Single mom and gourmet cat food entrepreneur Colbie Summers thought she'd escaped her tiny California hometown forever. But when her father needs her, she packs up her adolescent son, their finicky feline, Trouble, and her budding business. She knows change is tough—but she doesn't expect it to be murder . . .

Between dealing with her newly rural life, her grumpy, sports-obsessed father, and preparing to showcase her products in the local Sunnyside Power Mom's trade show, Colbie has more on her plate than she bargained for. Luckily, she has her official taste-tester, Trouble, by her side to vet her *Meow-io Batali Gourmet Cat Food* line. Things look promising—until one of the Power Moms is found dead—with an engraved *Meow-io* specialty knife buried in her chest.

As the prime suspect, Colbie needs paws on the ground to smoke out who had means, motive, and opportunity among the networking mothers—including a husband-stealing Sofia Vergara lookalike. And the cat's still not out of the bag when a second violent death rocks the bucolic community. Trouble may have nine lives, but Colbie's only got one to clear her name and stop a killer from pulling off the purr-fect crime . . .

The Trouble with Murder

A Gourmet Cat Mystery

Kathy Krevat

LYRICAL PRESS
Kensington Publishing Corp.
www.kensingtonbooks.com

This book is dedicated to my father Jim Hegarty. He lived life fully and loved deeply, and will be missed by many.

Acknowledgments:

I'd like to thank Jessica Faust, my awesome agent for making my publishing dreams come true, and Tara Gavin, my wonderful editor, for saying "Yes" to Trouble and making this book so much better.

This book wouldn't exist without the help of my critique group, the Denny's Chicks: Barrie Summy and Kelly Hayes.

I would not be writing today if it wasn't for the gentle editing of my first critique group, Betsy, Sandy Levin and the late Elizabeth Skrezyna.

I can never express the gratitude I feel toward all of the family and friends who support my writing career:

Pat Sultzbach, Lee Hegarty, Manny and Sandy Krevat, Donna and Brian Lowenthal, Patty Disandro, Jim Hegarty Jr., Michael and Noelle Hegarty, Matthew and Madhavi Krevat, Jeremy and Joclyn Krevat, Lynne and Tom Freeley, Lori and Murray Maloney, David Kreiss and Nasim Bavar, Lori Morse, Amy Bellefeuille, Sue Britt, Cathie Wier, Joanna Westreich, Susan O'Neill and the rest of the YaYa's, my Mom's Night Out group, and my book club.

A special shout out to Terrie Moran, author of the Read 'em and Eat mystery series, for her friendship and encouragement, and to Dru Ann Love for her friendship and support of the cozy mystery community.

Special thanks to the following experts for unselfishly sharing their knowledge:

Sergeant Cathy Allister, San Diego Sheriff's Department
Jim Hegarty for website and technical assistance
Katie Smith, NewRoad Foods
Stephenie Caughlin, Seabreeze Organic Farm
Olga Brumm, Animal Artistry Grooming
Dr. Susan Levy, for her medical knowledge
Judy Twigg, for being a typo-finding guru

Mountains of gratitude and love to my brilliant, beautiful and creative daughters, Devyn and Shaina Krevat, and to Lee Krevat, the love of my life!

Chapter 1

A chicken rang the doorbell.

I stood in the open doorway, a little dumbfounded, and stared down at the beige bird with a mop of floppy feathers on its head that looked like a hat. The kind of hat women wore as a half joke to opening day at the horse races. How could it even see through that thing? And did it really just ring the doorbell?

Braving the mid-morning heat of Sunnyside, California, inland from downtown San Diego by twenty miles and what felt like twenty degrees hotter, I stuck my head out and looked up and down my dad's street. No teens were hanging around, giggling over their prank.

The chicken ruffled its whole body as if to say, "Yes, it was me." The *you idiot* was implied by the way it poked his beak toward me and then scratched its feet on the wooden porch floor.

"Right." I spoke out loud. To a chicken. I had to get out of the house more.

I'd been up since four in the morning, grinding various chicken parts and cooking them for my organic cat food business, and I was already tired. Maybe this was a poultry hallucination brought on by exhaustion. Or induced by guilt.

Maybe this was the king of the chicken underworld, seeking retribution for what was going on in my kitchen.

I shook my head. I had to stop reading so many of those horror novels my bloodthirsty twelve-year-old son, Elliott, couldn't get enough of.

My dad shuffled over to stand beside me, tugging his bathrobe tighter around his waist. "Hey, Charlie," he said.

I raised my eyebrows. He was talking to a bird too. "A boy bird?" I asked. Was that really the most important thing about the chicken on our doorstep?

The chicken ignored both of us, now finding the railing fascinating enough to peck.

"Of course he's a boy bird," he said, his Boston accent coming through. "He's one of Joss's Buff Laces."

"What?"

"His chickens. This is a Buff Laced Polish chicken," he said. "Look at that comb."

"Comb?" I asked.

"That foofy thing on the top of his head," he told me.

The comb in question was quite remarkable, but what did I know about chickens?

"How did it, he, make it to the doorbell?" I thought chickens didn't fly. Wasn't that the whole point of them? Food that can't fly away?

"Charlie was owned by some shrink at a college or something," he said, his normal morning mad-scientist hair almost matching the bird's.

As if to demonstrate, Charlie flapped his wings, getting enough lift to hop onto the planter with some drooping lavender in it. He stretched out his neck to poke his beak at the doorbell. It took a few tries but then he got it, tilting his head as though he was listening to the "Yankee Doodle" tune that made me grind my teeth every time I heard it, and then hopped down, looking up at me expectantly.

Maybe this one was some kind of X-Games chicken.

"Does he want a treat?" I asked my dad.

Then my cat, Trouble, gave a low warning snarl that Charlie seemed to recognize because he turned around and fluttered down the steps in half-flight-half-run. I grabbed Trouble just as she was about to chase after the poor bird, and handed her to my dad. "Take her," I said. "I'll make sure Charlie gets home."

Trouble had been an apartment cat and hadn't been very curious about the outside world until we moved out of the city to my dad's house. Now we had to make sure she didn't escape every time we opened a door.

My dad held Trouble with his hands outstretched, looking unsure. Which was probably because she was still in full battle mode and swatted at me as soon as she could twist around in his arms, screeching, *"Let me at 'em."*

Not really, but I knew what she meant.

"She'll calm down in a minute," I told my dad as I dashed after the chicken.

Charlie was sticking to the sidewalk, but headed in the opposite direction from his home. After the doorbell stunt, I imagined he knew his way around town. But it wasn't up to me to keep him safe on an adventure. I just wanted to get him back to his pen.

Within seconds, I was dripping with sweat and regretting not grabbing my sunglasses. The glare of the mid-morning sun irritated my eyes that already felt scratchy from lack of sleep.

I ran in front of Charlie and attempted to sheep-dog him back the other way. He scooted around me.

"Damnit," I said, and hustled to get past him. He must have decided it was a race because he started running, determined to reach his goal, whatever that was.

I got in front of him, my huffing and puffing making me realize I should get back to the gym, and yelled, "Shoo!" while waving my arms like a...like a chicken.

He came to a stop in the most theatrical, wings flapping, squawking protest the world had ever seen, and reversed course.

"Drama queen," I said, hoping he didn't keep up the complaining all the way back. I hadn't yet met our neighbor, Joss Hayden, but something made me think that a certified organic farmer might not like me upsetting his chicken. Of course, I'd heard all about him from my dad, who said he was the best neighbor ever, occasional chicken coop odor notwithstanding.

Joss had bought the farm a year before, kept to himself, didn't have any parties, and didn't borrow any tools. I'd only seen a glimpse of him from a distance and imagined him to be some eccentric hippy, or even worse, a hipster dude getting back to nature. He grew organic vegetables in addition to his free-range chicken business.

Elliott had become a fan of Joss too, although that was probably more about visiting the baby chicks than the farmer himself.

It didn't take long for the traumatized chicken to scurry home, probably to blab to all his chicken friends about the torture he'd endured on his jaunt. The metal gates to the various pens were all locked. How did he get out? I was about to put him back in the closest one but realized he might belong somewhere else, so I went to the front door. Charlie followed along, hopping up the two steps to join me. Then the smart aleck ran across my foot, making me jump a bit, to ring the doorbell before I could. Joss the farmer was lucky enough to have a normal ding-dong doorbell. We both stood and waited.

A man wearing a black T-shirt answered the door with an annoyed expression. Even with the frown, he was attractive, in a non-hippy, non-hipster way. More like a *muscular-guy-who-puts-out-a-fire-and-then-drives-off-on-a-motorcycle* way. He looked from Charlie to me and his expression became confused. "You're not Charlie."

Ah, he must be a constant victim of the button-pushing. "Nope. Charlie rang my doorbell, and I brought him back." I held out my hand and then remembered that they'd been wrist deep in chicken livers. Even though I'd worn gloves to my elbows, it felt inappropriate. I pulled my hand back. "Colbie Summers. I'm, uh, helping out my dad a bit."

He'd reached out to shake my hand and it hung out there, shake-less.

"I've been handling…meat," I explained.

He smiled, as if figuring out I'd been holding chicken parts. "For your cat food business," he said. The wrinkles around his eyes deepened, and I noticed how blue they were.

Whoa. That was a nice smile. "Um, yes," I said, practically stuttering. "This batch is just for taste-testing. Not by me. By Trouble. You know. My cat." Although I had been known to try a few of the recipes. "The food I sell is actually made in a commercial kitchen." *Stop talking,* I told myself.

Charlie seemed to lose interest and jumped back down the steps.

"Your dad told me about Trouble," he said, keeping an eye on the chicken. "Sorry about the whole doorbell thing. Charlie was used for some kind of psychology experiments by his previous owner and will poke at anything button-like."

"It's okay," I said.

He shook his head as he came out and closed the door. "I don't know how he gets out all the time. He's the best escape artist I ever had." He walked to the edge of the porch. "It must be the trough. It's too close to the fence but I'd need a crane to move it."

From that viewpoint the farm was picture perfect—its large red barn painted with white trim, a green tractor parked beside old-fashioned gas tanks, and the chickens scratching in the pens. "Sorry," I said. "Don't have one of those with me." I turned to go. "Nice meeting you. Good luck with Charlie." I wasn't going to tell him that I couldn't leave my chicken livers marinating in green curry very long or the flavor would be too intense for my feline customers.

"Nice to meet you," he said. "You want to see the chicks before you rush back?"

"Um…" Was that how a chicken farmer made his move? I did a quick inventory of what I looked like. Cut off shorts to deal with the heat, a Padres Tshirt stained with meat juice, flip-flops, and a rolled-up bandana around my light brown hair with the copper stripe I needed to revive. And, oh yeah, red-rimmed eyes and no makeup. I was definitely safe from any moves by the farmer. And who could resist chicks? "Sure."

He jogged down the porch steps and walked back to the pen, scooping up Charlie as he opened the gate, and setting him down inside a pen by himself. Some chickens in the next section moved closer as if to check out the action. "In here," Joss said.

I walked carefully through the pen, watching where I put my feet. The door to the chicken coop was open and a few birds sat in nests. Then he opened a door inside and we were in some kind of incubator room. An orchestra of chick peeps reached a crescendo and an overwhelming chicken poop scent whooshed by.

"Whoa," I said, plugging my nose and then looking over apologetically.

"Sorry," he said cheerfully. "It takes a little getting used to."

When Joss moved closer, the chirping became even louder.

"So, the chicks love you," I said, not being able to resist the pun.

He looked startled for a second until he realized I was joking. "These are a bit too young for me."

I moved closer to the raised wooden beds with high sides holding the chicks. Heat lamps shone on them, even when it was so hot outside, and the brown and black fuzz balls moved closer to us. "They're adorable," I said. "They don't look like Charlie."

"No," Joss said. "They're Ameraucanas. They lay blue eggs." He picked one up gently. "Here." He put the baby chick in my cupped hands.

I couldn't help but say, "Aw."

And then it pooped. Right in my hand.

"Oops," he said. "Occupational hazard."

And then it pooped again.

"Let me—" he started, and I gladly tipped the chick into his hands. For some reason, I kept my hands together to prevent the mess from escaping, even though there was plenty on the floor.

He gently placed the creature back in its home, and pulled a wet wipe from a handy container hanging high above chicken level by the back door. "Here," he repeated, his eyes laughing at me.

"I got it." I grabbed the wipe, cleaning my hands as quickly as I could. "I'm a mom," I said a little defensively. "A little poop doesn't bother me." Of course, chicken poop was a different story. "I better get back." *To wash my hands with bleach.*

He opened the back door and I walked outside, the sun accosting my eyes again. Then I hit something slimy, sliding a whole two feet and wind-milling my arms before coming to a halt.

I looked down.

A hose had leaked, creating a slimy puddle of mud and chicken poop, which was now slopped all over my flip flops that were pointing in different directions, my feet solidly in the mess.

This time, Joss looked chagrined. "Sorry, sorry. I meant to replace that...." He looked at my feet as if not knowing what to do, and then bit his lip, trying not to smile.

"I'll..." *Burn these* didn't seem nice to say out loud. "Just go..."

"Yeah," he said, valiantly holding back laughter.

Men never outgrow poop humor.

I walked back to my dad's house, futilely attempting to scrape the mess off my flip flops onto the tiny patches of grass that lined the sidewalks. That was sticky stuff.

My dad's street looked like it could be in a seventies sitcom, with neat row houses, all the same white stucco walls and red clay tile roofs. Small driveways led to separate two car garages in the back, usually used for storage or workshops. Every yard hosted a few palm trees and a dried-out lawn that wasn't doing a good job surviving the summer drought regulations. The houses on my dad's side backed up to a huge family farm. The farmer had refused to sell to developers, so my dad had the best of both worlds. The convenience of all things suburbia and a wonderful view of open farmland. Of course, that open farmland smelled strongly of fertilizer at times, but it was worth it.

I tossed my disgusting flip flops and the poop-covered wipe in the garbage and used the garden hose to clean my feet before heading inside.

"Your phone rang," my dad called out from the living room over the sound of *Storage Wars*, his favorite show.

I grabbed my cell and headed back to the stove, tripping over the now-loving cat who wound around my ankles and purred, clearly saying, "*I wuv you so much. Isn't it time to taste test?*"

My Meowio Batali Gourmet Cat Food was marketed as organic food for the discerning cat, and many of my customers welcomed the most exotic of spices. But if Trouble didn't like it, I dropped it. I'd learned early on that she never steered me wrong. If she liked it, it sold. If she didn't like it, other cats didn't either.

My whole business was inspired by Trouble. I'd found her, not even six weeks old, abandoned in an apartment when a tenant skipped out on the rent. Elliott and I immediately fell in love with her tiny orange face and white paws, and adopted her. Because of the splash of white on her chest, Elliott had originally wanted to call her Skimbleshanks, after a cat character in the musical *Cats*.

She'd had a lot of digestive problems, and the only food she could handle was what I made. That, combined with her natural kitten mischievousness, earned her the name Trouble.

Soon, friends started asking to buy little jars of the same food for their cats, which is how I learned that there was a demand for organic, human-grade cat food. I increased my production, cooking at odd hours when I could sneak it in around my job managing the apartment building where we lived.

When I'd tried to expand to farmers' markets, I learned there were a lot of regulations I'd have to follow to make it a real business, including cooking all the food sold at the market in a certified kitchen.

My previous customers still demanded my original products, including the cute packaging, so I spent at least one morning a week indulging them. Their cats had benefitted from me learning how to add vitamins and other goodies to make the food more nutritious.

I'd already been up for hours cooking and packaging my Chicken & Sage Indulgence. The herbal smell bothered Elliott and my dad, so I liked to get the kitchen aired out before they even woke up. Trouble absolutely loved that recipe–she'd come running the moment the sage hit the sizzling olive oil and yelled at me to give her tidbits the whole time I was cooking. When I was done with production, I switched to trying new recipes.

My phone had a message from my best friend, Lani, but I had to finish up the chicken liver curry dish before calling her back. I'd also received an alert that someone had given my business a review on SDHelp. I clicked over to the site and saw that a J. Greene had given me one star!

I opened the app to read the review. *I bought this cat food at the local flea market—*

Flea market? It's a farmers' market, idiot. There's a big difference. I read on.

I had high hopes for this locally-produced, organic cat food, but my cat took one bite and walked away. I couldn't taste it–even I don't love my cat that much–but I sniffed it and it smelled awful. A combination of chemicals and rotten meat. Will never buy again.

What? That was impossible. I'd never had a bad review like this. Once someone complained about the price, but I'd never be able to compete price-wise with the big guys. What should I do? Ignore it? Contact Mr. J. Greene and offer to replace it?

I put a few pieces of curried chicken into the refrigerator to cool while I mentally ran through my process. Since my dad got sick, I hadn't always been in the commercial kitchen the two mornings a week I could afford to rent, relying on my cook who always followed my instructions meticulously.

Could something have gone wrong with one batch? But then I would hear from more than one customer. I clicked on the website to see if anyone had left a complaint there. Nothing. I took a deep breath. Maybe it was an isolated incident. Or total bull.

To reassure myself, I turned to the page that had testimonials from my customers. So many of them noted how much healthier their cats were because they ate Meowio food.

"Mom!" Elliott yelled as he ran down the stairs, landing at the bottom with a thud. My son rarely did anything quietly.

I met him in the hall while my dad silenced the TV and stuck his head out to see what was going on.

"I got a callback for Horton!" Elliott announced as he threw his arms in the air in triumph and then fell on the floor in a dramatic faint, clutching his phone to his chest.

"That's awesome," I said, pushing back the guilt that I'd totally forgotten about his audition for theater summer camp. Starting on Monday, he'd be spending two weeks with a bunch of other drama kids on a musical—his idea of heaven. On the last Friday, the whole camp would perform *Seussical the Musical*. "Isn't Horton one of the leads?" The musical incorporated a couple of Dr. Seuss books into one plot including *Horton Hears a Who*.

Elliott rolled himself up and jumped to his feet, his dark brown hair flopping over one eye. "Yes!"

"Congratulations, kid," I said, delighted for him. "When's the audition?"

He clicked on his phone, reading farther down the email he'd received. His face fell. "Uh-oh," he said. "It's this Thursday afternoon."

That was one of my farmers' market days and my biggest sales day. My best customers knew they could find me every Thursday afternoon in downtown San Diego, selling my cat food with Trouble watching over the booth in her little chef hat. I'd already paid for my prime spot.

I forced a smile. "It's okay," I said. "We'll just go to the market late."

"I can take him," my dad called out from the living room.

Elliott's eyes widened and he shook his head in a silent plea.

Oh man. I had to handle this carefully. "It's okay, Dad. I love going to Elliott's auditions," I said in a light tone. "And he can help me at the market afterward."

He subsided with a "harrumph." Normally having my dad drive Elliott might work, but he hadn't driven much since he got out of the hospital. And this was Elliott's first time auditioning for the Sunnyside Junior Theater, and he didn't know anyone. Even when Elliott tried out for his old theater group where he felt comfortable, he had to be managed carefully so he went into his audition feeling confident. And my dad hadn't been very supportive of anything Elliott did that wasn't sports-related.

Elliott let out his breath. He and my dad had gotten along on our short visits over the years, but hadn't found much common ground since we'd moved in. My dad wouldn't admit to needing help after his second devastating bout with pneumonia. My macho, football-playing father hated being weak and being forced to accept support from the same daughter he'd driven out of the house thirteen years ago.

And he wouldn't say it out loud, but it was clear he wasn't happy with Elliott's fashion choices. Especially the way Elliott shaved one side of his head and allowed the other to grow long. From the photos of my own grunge days in high school, I knew Elliott would regret that look in the future, but he had to make his own fashion mistakes.

"The director sent me the sheet music for 'Alone in the Universe,' and I only have two days to learn it. I'm gonna go practice." Elliott ran back up to his room, taking the stairs a couple at a time.

"Break a leg!" I called after him. I smiled, caught up in his enthusiasm.

Until my dad "harrumphed" again from the living room.

I took a deep breath, determined to let my dad's bad attitude go. *He's sick*, I told myself and headed back to the kitchen.

But he didn't stop. "I don't know why you let him do that nonsense," he said, lighting my simmering anger.

I did a U-turn at the kitchen doorway and stomped into the living room. "What nonsense? Having fun with other kids? Developing his talents? Pursuing a dream?"

My dad scowled. "Singing and dancing's not preparing him for the future."

"He's twelve, Dad," I said sarcastically. "He has time. And you think playing with a ball on a field prepares him for the future?"

"It sure does," he said, defensive. "It teaches teamwork. And following the rules. Something both of ya could learn." He sat back in his chair, and suddenly he seemed smaller in it. Had he lost more weight?

My anger washed out of me. "He loves it, Dad," I said, my voice calmer. "And there's a heck of a lot of teamwork going on behind the scenes and on stage." I'd seen it first-hand during the obligatory volunteering that went along with any kind of youth theater.

He narrowed his eyes, as if trying to figure out if I was just feeling sorry for him. Then he turned the TV sound back on with his remote. *Storage Wars* characters were trying to goad each other into bidding higher on someone's junk.

"It's a good thing my investments are paying off so I can help with his college," he grumbled as I took a step to the door. "My new fund is up a full twenty percent this month."

"What?" I asked. "You have investments?"

"Of course I have investments," he said, bristling again. "You think I'm an idiot?"

"No," I said. I couldn't imagine having enough money for "investments." "You're helping with Elliott's college?"

"Of course I am," he said. "He's not getting a singing scholarship, is he?"

I gaped at him. That comment had so many levels of insult that I couldn't think of a retort to cover them all.

Luckily my phone rang before any sound could come out of my mouth. I counted to ten on the way back to the kitchen and answered it.

"Oh. My. God," Lani said, her voice breaking up a little over her car Bluetooth connection. "I'm gonna kill Piper."

"Good morning to you too," I said. Piper was her wife and Lani threatened to kill her about once a week, usually for no good reason.

I pulled out the now cool pieces of chicken curry and put them in Trouble's dish. She sniffed it, and then took a bite. Her lips curled back as she chewed. Then she spit it out.

Shoot. There goes that recipe. Unless I tried it again with less curry?

"She threw out my latest prototype! On purpose!" I heard Lani's car engine zoom in the background, as if it was angry at Piper too.

Lani was the owner and creator of Find Your Re-Purpose, an online boutique of unique baby fashions recycled from used clothing. She cut up old clothing, sewed different materials together, added some fabric paint or other touches, and voila! A beautiful, one-of-a-kind, hundred dollar outfit that anyone with too much money could buy for a baby who would most likely spit up on it in less than five minutes.

We'd met years before when she was the costume designer for one of Elliott's plays, and quickly figured out that she lived in my dad's neighborhood. After a few sleepless nights of last minute costume adjustments before the show's opening, we'd become best friends.

"Was it that cape idea you were kicking around?" I asked.

"Yes!" she said. "It was the cutest thing EV-ER!"

I'd had my own doubts about the safety of capes for infants, but had kept them to myself. Since Piper was a pediatrician, I knew she'd step in. "Where are you headed?" I asked, trying to distract her.

"Ventura," she said. "A thrift shop just got a big donation of clothes from a rich European family who spent the last six months in Malibu. The material has a bunch of cool designs the shop owner has never seen before so he put them aside for me. I can't wait to see them."

Ventura was almost four hours from Sunnyside, which meant Lani would be gone most of the day. Since she liked company on her trip, I put her on speaker phone right by the stove, resumed my stirring, and settled in for a long conversation.

"Have you heard from Twomey's yet?" she asked, with a change in her tone that meant *now-it's-time-for-friendly-nagging*. She'd encouraged me to contact the local chain of seven organic food stores offering my cat food products.

"Not yet," I admitted. In my e-mail, I'd pushed the fact that buying local was all the rage, especially for the kind of people who bought organic products to help save the planet.

Seeing Meowio Batali products on the shelves of that many stores would be a dream come true. But I wasn't sure how I'd meet any significant increase in demand without hiring more people. And that took money.

I was pretty stretched already—both physically and money-wise. Too bad cloning me wasn't an option yet. If I had two, maybe three more of me, I could do everything I should be doing.

I changed the subject. "Hey, I finally met my neighbor."

"That cute chicken farmer?" she asked.

I turned on the frying pan and dribbled in extra virgin olive oil. "How'd you know he was cute?"

"Everyone knows he's cute," she said. "He's also single, keeps to himself and hasn't dated at all."

"Good to know," I said. I told her all about the chicks and the unfortunate poop incident.

"That's such a meet cute!" she said. "You can tell your grandchildren that story where you fell in love with his chicks first."

"I think if there's poop involved, it's the exact opposite of a meet cute," I said. "And I really don't have time to date right now."

"You know, it's really a little like Romeo and Juliet, except with your cat and chickens," she said. "Joss is a Montague and you're the Cat-ulets." She giggled at her own joke.

"And you know how they ended up." I tossed chunks of chicken in the pan. "Hey, did you head out of town on purpose so I couldn't drag you to my Power Moms trade show?"

"Oh yeah," she said unapologetically. "It's the only reason I chose today to drive to freakin' Ventura. Just to get away from your cult."

I laughed. The Sunnyside Power Moms, or SPMs for short, was a group of home business owners who worked together to network and support each other. Our leader, Twila Jenkins, got the idea to start the group when the third mom came up to her at the Sunnyside Elementary School playground to invite her to a party at her house. One of those "parties" where the host/salesperson puts out lovely hors d'oeuvres and lots of wine so that her guests, i.e., sales targets, will feel more inclined to buy thirty dollar candles and forty-five dollar candle holders.

Twila had invited me to join after learning about my cat food business.

"You'll come around," I said. "The first step was when you suggested your friend Fawn become an SPM. You're one step closer to becoming One of Us. One of Us." I chanted that in a low tone a few times until she interrupted me.

"Not a chance," she said. "Hey! You should manufacture some kind of scandal. That'll get people interested in your little coven."

I rolled my eyes, even though she couldn't see me. "Be nice or I'll sign you up to host a candle party at your house."

She gasped dramatically. "A fate worse than death."

Chapter 2

A fate worse than death.

I couldn't help but remember Lani's words when I was attacked by a gang of rabid soccer moms waiting outside the activity center in Twila's gated community. Twila had given the gate code to everyone, but she'd given only me the key code to the building. I was totally on time, but that wasn't enough for these over-achievers.

With everyone waiting by my shoulder, I fumbled a few times as I entered it, and finally got it right. Each digit played a musical note and then the door buzzed.

"Sounds like Beethoven's Fifth," one of the moms said. "*Bump-bump-bump-buzz*," she repeated, blaring out the last note.

I laughed, probably from nerves, and we went inside, ready to set up. It was a good thing I'd taken a nap and picked up an extra-large coffee to prepare for the trade show.

We'd all pitched in to rent the banquet hall, a large round room with windows looking out over the golf course. Somehow because of my experience at farmers' markets, I'd been put in charge of assigning all the booths—a thankless task—and creating the SPM Scavenger Hunt—another thankless task. Guests who visited each of our booths and got a stamp inked on the form could win a grand prize of a basket full of goodies from all the vendors.

I wasn't sure how the evening would play out so I'd left Trouble at home. Bronx Innis stopped me as I was unloading boxes. "I need electrical tape!" she said. She had a mobile pet grooming business, and had come up with the idea of a puppy petting booth for the trade show. "There are extension cords running right through my space."

"I have a roll in my car," I reassured her. My farmers' market experience was paying off. "I'll bring it over."

Then Daria Valdez grabbed my arm. I fumbled my box and nearly dumped my cans of assorted Meowio Batali food.

"Sorry," she said, "But my booth can NOT be near Mona's." Her face was red with anger. Then she took a deep breath and spoke more calmly. "We have competing products, so it makes more sense to keep us far apart."

Daria was a BeesWax Party consultant, marketing the overpriced candles Lani and I laughed about, and Mona Hayworth ran Spicy Parties selling massage oils, lingerie, and other "adult" products.

Mona strolled over, and I realized the real problem. In keeping with her risqué goods, she was wearing a black satin robe that was more suited for the Playboy Mansion than a family trade show.

Before Mona could say anything, Gina Pace rushed in front of her. "Why am I all the way in the back?" she asked, flipping her blond ponytail over her shoulder. "I'll get no traffic at all." Gina ran, literally, the Mommy and Me exercise classes where moms with babies in joggers dashed all over Sunnyside, losing their pregnancy weight at record speed.

I decided to tackle the easy one first. "You are right beside the raffle ticket box and free refreshments," I told Gina. "Everyone will walk by."

"Oh. Okay, fine," she said, and jogged back toward her booth, knees high, totally ignoring the Daria-Mona drama.

I turned to the woman who looked so much like Sofia Vergara she could be her slightly older stunt double. "Mona, is there something…less revealing you can wear from your product line?" When she slammed her eyebrows together, I added, "You look absolutely *gorgeous*, but there are bound to be children here, and we don't want to offend any potential customers."

Since I was the youngest in the group by far, I had to walk a fine line. I may have just stepped over it.

She pursed her lips as if considering, and then gave us both an elaborate shrug. "I'll see what I can do." She pushed her hair over her shoulder and turned around, in the sexy walk of a classic Hollywood movie star. Or Jessica Rabbit.

"I'm sure she won't be pushing her candles tonight," I reassured Daria when she was out of earshot. "Not wearing something like that."

She scowled after her, her dark eyes flashing. "She'll be pushing—" She cut herself off with a short shake of her head. "I'll deal."

I sighed and walked to my own table, while Twila arrived with a large box, and plopped it on the table right beside mine. "Isn't this exciting?" she said before going back outside for another box. With her freckles and curly red hair cut asymmetrically, she made me think of a 1920's flapper girl.

Twila was the SoCal Puzzle Lady. Soon she was setting up children's wooden puzzles of farm animals, organizing jigsaw puzzles by number of pieces, and stacking 3D metal brainteasers, probably according to how crazy someone gets trying to solve them. She even put up a backdrop—a wall-sized crossword puzzle.

"Have you done this before?" I asked her, as she carefully placed an Einstein bust on a table.

"A few times," she said.

No wonder she knew to avoid table placement responsibility.

"Do you know who was responsible for the gate?" she asked. "It wasn't propped open, and I can't remember who volunteered."

"Sorry, I don't."

She shrugged. "I took care of it."

I started arranging my newest product line, a butcher block full of knives and a set of kitchen utensils with cute cat paw prints engraved on them. They were an expensive investment, but had become a nice addition to my cat food income. I put the knife set on the table behind me, out of reach of curious children.

Sharon Merritt, owner of Chaos Commando, a closet organization company whose brochure photos of perfectly organized closets always made me envious, stopped over. She was probably itching to rearrange my pyramid of Fish Romance to perfectly match the pile of Chicken Sauté. "Is your Square working?" she asked, holding up her cell phone with the white square attachment that most of us were using for credit card sales.

Daria called out, "I was having trouble earlier, but now it's fine."

Sharon tried again, frowning at her phone. "There it is! Thank you, dear." She had a round face with a perpetually worried expression. I'd made the mistake of telling Lani that she looked like a matronly angel troubled about her flock, and that's all she could talk about for a week when I brought up the group.

"No problem," Daria replied.

I got back to organizing my booth with a sigh of relief.

Soon we had a decent crowd of friends and neighbors, with almost all the booths getting some trade show action. Many guests held coupons that some of the moms must have sent out ahead of time for special offers. Mona had a line of sheepish looking men at her booth. I couldn't wait to find out what kind of coupon she'd sent out.

Twila had offered a big discount on a small jigsaw puzzle of a lit-up New York Broadway scene. "Save me one of those," I told her. "Elliott'll like it."

"Sure thing," she said.

"Hey, in case someone complains later," I started, and told her about the issue Daria had with Mona.

Twila shook her head. "Yeah, that problem's brewing for a while."

"So I handled it okay?" I asked.

"Yes. It's between them," she said. "But if it's going to spill over to the group, we'll have a meeting to deal with it." She turned back to prevent a young child from toppling the glowing globe on her table.

The next two hours flew by and before long only a few customers lingered. I'd sold out of several of my flavors and handed out dozens of cards advertising my website.

Twila was about to walk around the activity center to take an informal survey of the event when a group of late-arriving teachers stopped at her booth. "Can you see what everyone thought?" she asked me. "I'll keep an eye on your booth." She handed over a clipboard with a sheet of paper and all the SPM members' names typed up with "Notes" beside them.

I couldn't imagine that level of organization.

Daria had regained her normal good humor and was ecstatic about her sales. I peeked at the price of a small tea light holder in the shape of an owl. Forty dollars! If she was selling a bunch of those, no wonder she was happy.

Mona was pleased as well, but didn't give any details. She had what looked like a large genie bottle full of forms with names and addresses of people interested in her parties.

Sharon said she'd handed out business cards and needed to schedule appointments with people interested in closet organization. "Next time we do something like this, you should take registrations and get e-mails from everyone, not just those who stopped by a booth."

I hadn't had much interaction with Sharon before, but I'd learned early that she loved to give advice. Maybe because she was the only empty-nester in the group and didn't have kids at home to advise anymore. Or maybe that's what made her a great closet organizer—she was good at telling people what to do.

Bronx, the owner of SoCal Spaw, bubbled over with delight. "I met SO many new potential customers!" she said, her southern accent more pronounced in her excitement. "With my trade show coupon, they can get me at the same price as most regular groomers. For the first time anyway." The puppies she'd brought were all sleeping in two small crates.

"Great strategy." I admired her flyers with pink and purple cartoon drawings of a dog with a bow in its hair and a smiling cat.

Beside them was a stack of black business cards with only the words *Lice Club Lady* and a phone number in silver font. "Who's this?" I asked.

"I don't know," she said. "They just appeared there during the evening."

I turned the card over. *What happens in the Lice Club stays in the Lice Club.* "Did you see the back?" I handed it to her.

"Ooh," she said. "That's so weird. But, you know, clever."

I agreed, and put the card in my pocket. Maybe the Lice Club Lady wanted to join our little group. I certainly hoped I wouldn't need her services. Elliott was out of elementary school but I'd heard even middle schools sometimes had outbreaks.

Next stop was Fawn Escanso's booth where she was advertising her website design business and her new life coach practice, and requesting donations for her nonprofit that found jobs for kids graduating from the foster youth program. On top of raising four boys. She must never sleep.

Before I could talk to her, I saw Twila waving at me with my phone in her hand. "I heard your cell ringing twice," she said when I walked back to her. "I tried to answer, but I didn't catch it in time. Sorry to be nosy, but I could see at least one text from Elliott."

I took the phone from her and the screen held the beginnings of several texts from my son. *When are you going to get home??? Grandpa is coughing like crazy and I'm worried!!* Elliott had added a few emojis of someone turning green. I wasn't sure if he meant my dad or himself. My concern must have shown on my face.

"Everything okay?" Twila asked.

I bit my lip. "Elliott says my dad is coughing hard again."

"You go ahead home," she said. "I'm the clean-up committee anyway so I'll bring your boxes to your house."

"No, that's okay," I said. "This stuff is heavy."

"Colbie," she said, her voice all serious. "I went through this when my mom was sick. When a friend offers to help you, they truly want you to say 'yes.'"

I blinked at her a moment, feeling overwhelmed by emotion. She'd called me out on my secret fear—of ever needing help. And my even more secret wish to have friends who would offer. "Okay. Yes. And thanks."

"You're welcome," she said. "Now get out of here." She waved her hands toward the door in a *get going* gesture.

"Thank you," I said over my shoulder. I went back to my table and threw my cash box and receipt book into my large shoulder bag and left.

* * * *

By the time I got home, Trouble was waiting at the door and my dad had a glass of whiskey in his hand, his cure-all for almost any illness. He'd stopped coughing, but was cursing at his computer.

"What's wrong?" I asked, lifting Trouble into my arms and holding her like a baby. She rested a paw on my chin and purred, which had to mean *I'm so glad you're home.* I looked over my dad's shoulder while he sat at his makeshift desk on a corner display table in the living room. He had a small office upstairs but I'd moved his laptop and desk chair down when he got sick.

"This website is screwed up," he said. "I'm trying to move my money and it's saying I can't."

"Your bank?"

"No," he said, frustration in his voice. "That investment account I told you about. I decided to get out while I was ahead, but their website is saying I don't have the right to move it."

"Do you want me to look at it?" I asked.

"No," he said. "I'm going to call my guy."

My stomach tightened at the words *my guy.* My dad had a distrust of companies and believed they charged more than they should. He'd had "my guy" for everything from the amateur bee removal "expert" who had to come out five times to remove a hive, to the contractor who'd started an add-on to our house and then took off for parts unknown with my dad's deposit, leaving behind a doorway to nowhere from the laundry room.

"Who is he?" I asked, trying to sound relaxed. But then I added, "Are you sure he's legit?"

"Of course he's legit." He flicked through his phone contact list. "It's Bert Merritt. He's married to that closet woman."

Closet woman? "Sharon?" I asked.

"Yeah." He put the phone on speaker.

"Bert here," a man answered.

"Bert!" my dad yelled and gave me a look that said *See. And you doubted my guy.* "I'm trying to move some money out, and I was having trouble with your website."

"Trouble?" he said. "No one else has said anything. Probably because no one in their right mind would get out now." He added a little laugh that was probably meant to soften the insult.

I raised my eyebrows at my dad, but he didn't notice. "I'd normally ride it out," my dad said, "but it's a good time, when I've already got so much return."

"Yeah, but it's still going up," Bert said, all smarm. "You're too smart to get out when it's about to take off even more."

My dad frowned, not liking being told no. "Perhaps, but I still need the money. Not the entire amount of course."

"Maybe my tech guy has the website down for maintenance." I heard Bert type in a three-digit key code and a deep buzz that sounded familiar. "I'll give him a call and you can try again in a few—"

The voice cut out.

"Hello?" My dad waited. Then he swore and redialed. It went straight to message. "He must not have cell service where he is."

The key code and the buzz. It had sounded just like Beethoven's Fifth. "I think he's at the activity center," I said.

"What?" he asked.

"At the trade show I left a little while ago," I said. "It sounds like the same key code for the door. Maybe he's helping Sharon pack up."

"Really?" he asked, as if he didn't quite believe me. "Did your phone work there?"

"Yep," I said. "I don't think anyone had trouble."

"I want this taken care of tonight," he said, his jaw set to "stubborn." Then he redialed. It went straight to voice mail. He narrowed his eyes at me. "Let's go over there."

"The activity center?" I asked.

"Yes." He stood up. "You said you recognized the security code. The Beethoven thing or whatever. I think he's trying to avoid me."

"It's twenty minutes away," I said. "Even if I'm right, he could be gone when we get there."

To answer, my dad redialed the number and stared at me, his expression mulish.

Voice mail.

I sighed. "Okay."

* * * *

After letting Elliott know we'd be back soon and plopping Trouble onto my dad's chair, I headed back to Twila's gated community with my dad in the passenger seat.

We sat in awkward silence until he asked in an *oh-so-casual* voice, "So how's the business going?" He was staring out the window. Was he trying to show me it was no big deal or that he didn't want to scare me off with questions?

And why did every serious conversation with him have to be fraught with so many emotional landmines?

"Good," I replied, hoping he wasn't going to pipe up with advice. "I'm waiting to hear from Twomey's. If they're at all interested in selling my food in their stores, they'll ask for a business proposal."

"They'd be idiots not to," he said gruffly. "But you already work so hard at all hours. How are you going to do even more?"

I took a deep breath, telling myself that he was concerned and not questioning my judgment. "I've been saving a little, and if I get the deal, I'll figure it out. I'm hoping my cook can give me more hours if I need her."

He was silent a minute as we arrived back at Twila's community. "Back in the city?"

I pushed the button to open my window as I drove up the keypad sticking out from the wall. I typed in the gate code and it opened with a metallic groan. "I'm not sure yet," I said, keeping my tone neutral.

"Maybe they have one of those commercial kitchens out this way," he said. "Might even be cheaper."

I caught my breath. Was he hinting that he wanted us to stay? "Might be."

He stayed quiet as we drove the rest of the way to the activity center. The lights were still on inside, but the visitor parking lot was empty except for a lonely golf cart. We both got out of the car. Palm trees rustled above us, driven by a breeze too high for us to feel. A few house lights blinked from across the golf course.

"Looks like they're all gone," I said.

"Let's go make sure," my dad said.

Did he need money that bad all of a sudden? "What's the rush on the money?" I asked.

He frowned. "I have a few ideas."

We walked up the short path, pausing a minute at the glass door. Inside I could see dark footprints heading toward us. "What the heck is that?"

"Just open it and let's see if Bert's in the back or something," my dad said, too impatient to pay attention.

I typed in the code and the door buzzed. Definitely Beethoven.

I opened the door and my dad brushed by me. Then he stopped abruptly. "What is this?"

The footprints came from the back of the banquet room, where my table had been. They were red.

"Is that blood?" Without thinking, I knelt down and touched an imprint. "Oh my God!" I jumped up and took a step. A smell came from the room, something that I recognized at some instinctive level, and my heart started pounding.

"Damnit, Colbie!" he said, grabbing my arm. "Someone could still be in here!"

I pulled away. "And someone could be hurt." I avoided walking on the footprints, and followed them.

Right to the body of Twila Jenkins.

Her arms were thrown back against the floor as if she was still trying to back away from danger.

A Meowio Batali butcher knife was buried in her chest.

Chapter 3

I dropped to one knee, panic making me lightheaded.

"Colbie!" my dad yelled as I disappeared, a table blocking his view.

"I'm okay," I said weakly. "Call 911." I shook my head and stood up.

Blood had spread through nooks and crannies in the hardwood floor, coming to rest in a large pool.

"Already waiting for the damn fools to pick up," he said. I heard his labored breathing as he moved closer. He put a hand on my shoulder. "I'd like to report a dead body." Then he asked, "She's dead, right?"

I took a deep breath and forced myself to move closer. I reached down to feel Twila's neck, knowing there was no chance. No pulse. "Yeah. She's dead."

My eyes went to the bloody footprints that started at the other side of the body. Someone had stayed around long enough to let enough blood soak into their shoes to track it all the way outside. What kind of monster did this?

Then the back service door to the banquet room opened and someone whispered, "Holy crap."

I turned around to see a frightened young man in a security uniform staring at me. His hand fumbled at his side.

I put my hands up, just like on TV.

And just like on TV, he yelled, "Freeze!"

* * * *

The security guard had been reaching for his walkie-talkie. Why did those things still exist when there were cell phones? Within minutes, the police arrived with lights flashing and sirens wailing. My dad and I were escorted to separate picnic tables outside the activity center to wait for someone to take our statements while an officer wound crime scene tape around the whole activity center. I sat in stunned silence.

It seemed like hours before a San Diego Sheriff car pulled up. A woman got out wearing street clothes but with an air of command that made the officer who had arrived first stand a little straighter while he answered her questions. She was about my height, with short dark hair that she pulled behind her ears and a thin face. She looked both my dad and me up and down, and then directed her partner to talk to my dad while she swung her legs over the bench to sit across from me at my table. I felt like I was somehow thrust into the middle of a movie and couldn't get out.

"Are you okay?" the woman officer asked me in a concerned yet professional voice. She must have to ask that a lot.

I nodded. "Yes, Officer." My voice was shaky.

"It's Detective, but you can call me Norma," she said. "It's just a formality, but I need to read you your rights."

I nodded, her calm recitation of the Miranda rights feeding into the sense that this couldn't be happening to me.

The deputy talking to my dad looked like a tough guy, holding himself erect even on the picnic table bench. His biceps were so big they forced his arms away from his sides.

"You play ball?" I heard my dad ask, and I knew he'd bond with the guy over sports and be okay.

Norma jerked her head toward the residents gathering behind the tape, and a younger officer responded by turning the video camera he was holding toward them. She turned back to me. "Can you tell me what happened here?"

"I don't know," I said. "I had to leave in a hurry and Twila offered to clean up for me. When I came back, she was...like that." My mind couldn't wrap itself around what I'd just seen. How could Twila be dead? What would her husband do? Her kids?

"The security guard said there was some kind of event here tonight."

I nodded. "The Sunnyside Power Moms—"

She raised her eyebrows. "Power Moms?"

"Yes. We're mothers who have home businesses, and we hosted a trade show tonight."

She took out her notepad. "What is your business?"

"I own Meowio Batali Gourmet Cat Food," I said. "One of my knives was used...."

"One of your knives was the murder weapon?"

"Well, one of the ones on display," I said. "I'd placed them on the back table to keep them away from kids."

She wrote that down and asked as if it wasn't important, "And why did you leave early?"

"My son texted me that my father had started coughing a lot," I explained. "He's getting over pneumonia, and I was worried."

She nodded once, communicating, "*Go on,*" without saying a word.

I explained about his conversation with Bert Merritt. "I heard the same beeps as the security code here, so we came back to talk to him. But he wasn't here."

She made a note. Probably *thinks she can tell security code sounds apart.*

"Why would your father's financial advisor be here?" Norma asked.

"He's married to Sharon, the closet lady," I said.

She raised her eyebrows.

"She builds closets and organizes people's stuff," I explained. I took a deep breath and tried to quiet my spinning mind. Then I gave her the list of moms who were at the event and their businesses. By the end, she looked a little overwhelmed. I didn't blame her. We were a pretty eclectic group.

"Back to the financial advisor," she said. "Was he here?"

I shook my head. "Not by the time we arrived."

"Does he know Twila?" Her voice was still calm, but I could sense where she was going.

"I don't know," I said, now panicking that I might be implicating my colleague's husband.

"How well do you know Twila?" she asked.

Oh man. I did not like the emphasis she put on "*you.*"

"She organized our group," I said. "She's, was, my friend." I bit my lip and for the first time, had to blink back tears. Twila was *dead.* How could this happen?

Norma stared at me, noticing my emotion, and then asked me all the same questions, but in different ways. After answering them again, I heard my dad's hacking cough. I looked over and he seemed pale. "Look, I'm happy to help you. Twila was really great to me. But my son is alone and my dad's still sick. I have to get him home to rest."

She looked like she wanted to object, but I stood up. "Dad," I called out. "Time to get back to Elliott."

The detective interviewing my dad jumped to his feet and stepped close, puffing out his chest in a blatant attempt to intimidate me. "I'm not done."

My dad coughed again, so hard he had to wrap his arms around his chest.

I gestured with my hand toward my dad. "He's recovering from pneumonia."

"It's okay," my dad choked out.

"No, it's not," I insisted. "I'm taking you home."

The policeman scowled, obviously ticked off that I was challenging his authority.

"Detective." Norma's voice held a command. "They can go."

He took a long moment to respond by taking a step back, and I could practically feel the anger emanating from him.

Norma turned to me and said, "We'll need you both to come downtown to make a statement first thing tomorrow."

I nodded, helped my dad to his feet, and we headed to the car. The officer made a big show of staring at the license plate of our car and writing it down on his notepad. Norma spoke to him while I was closing the door, and I hurried to open my window to hear what he said.

"This is just like the Wilson case," he said, his voice carrying in the quiet evening. "Open and shut."

* * * *

Elliott was both appalled and morbidly fascinated by Twila's murder. He'd met her once at the grocery store. She'd been wearing a Minecraft T-shirt, and they'd bonded over a mutual love of the game. Elliott had been totally impressed that she made a living doing something as cool as inventing puzzles.

No matter how I spun it, making cat food would never be cool.

"Did you see her...dead?" Elliott asked. He was trying to hold Trouble on his lap, but the cat had been on edge the whole time we'd been home, as if she'd caught our agitation.

"Not now," I said, while my dad coughed so hard in his chair I thought he was going to implode. I rushed to fill the whiskey glass and shoved it in his hand. "Do you need your inhaler?"

He shook his head, which meant he'd already used it too much today. As soon as he could breathe, he took a huge swig of the whiskey. "Thanks," he wheezed out.

"But what did you see?" Elliott asked again.

"Elliott Dean Summers," I said, focused on my dad. "If you don't stop asking me questions immediately—"

Luckily for me, he didn't force me to finish my threat, which was good because I didn't have a good consequence in mind yet. He groaned as if under terrible torture, let the cat jump to the floor, and then stomped up the stairs to his room. It was past his bedtime anyway.

"Curious little brat, isn't he?" my dad said, with enough affection in his voice that I wasn't offended. His breathing was still rough, but the coughing had stopped.

I sighed. "I read that's a good thing."

"It is," he said with a smile and then sobered. "I'm sorry about your friend."

What? We didn't do feelings in our house. I was suddenly overcome by sadness. Poor Twila. My breath caught in my throat. "I gotta…"

Then Trouble shot to the front door, her whole body on alert, at the same time I heard a noise. Normally, I'd think it was just a wild animal roaming around, but I was freaked out by finding Twila.

I stood up and my dad said, "Don't." He pulled his cell phone out of his pocket and dialed 911. Twice in one night—a new record for calling the police.

Trouble snarled at the same time the doorbell rang.

I froze.

My dad got to his feet to join me and gestured toward the kitchen. It had a window that looked out over the front porch where we could see who was at the door.

We moved together as he talked quietly to the dispatcher. "We have a prowler," he said, and gave the address. "Someone's at the front door. My daughter and I are going to look out a window and see who it is."

The person on the phone tried to dissuade him.

"No, we're not opening the door," he explained. "We're looking from a side window."

I tiptoed into the kitchen and pushed aside the curtain to see who was at our door so late at night.

Detective Norma and the detective who had talked to my dad.

Great.

Their police officer ESP must have been working overtime, because they turned together to see me at the window.

Detective Tough Guy shined his flashlight right at me. "Open the door," he demanded, his loud voice clear through the window. "Now."

* * * *

Norma must have reined in her partner, because he was scowling but silent when we opened the door. "We were hoping for a little more of your time," she said.

My dad started to say, "Sure," but I cut him off.

"What does that mean?" I asked.

"Detective Little and I were hoping to take a look around," she said. "With your permission of course."

Detective Little? I almost giggled. Probably because of nerves, but really, he must get a lot of jokes in the locker room.

"We got nothing to hide," my dad said, laying a hand on my arm.

"To keep the lawyers happy," she said, holding a form out to my dad, "could you sign this?"

"And we need your clothes," Detective Little said, with an edge to his voice that rubbed me the wrong way. "And shoes."

I went into sarcasm mode immediately. "I don't think they'd fit you," I managed, even though his determined expression was scaring the crap out of me.

Then Trouble joined in, making an unholy growl that sounded remarkably like "*Slytherin!*" and dashed straight at him. I grabbed her at the last second in mid-leap.

Since she was heading straight for Little's crotch, he let out a tiny squeal and crossed his hands in front of himself before recovering and glaring at both of us.

"Ms. Summers," Norma said in a no-nonsense tone. "Hold on to that cat or I will call Animal Control."

"Really?" I said, trying to quiet the squirming cat. "You know darn well we are cooperating fully and you threaten my cat?" I took the unsigned form out of my dad's hand. "We will give you our clothes and you can walk through with one of us present. Other than that, you get a warrant."

They both narrowed their eyes at me and then Norma spoke. "We're on the same side. We're just trying to catch a killer. So no one else gets hurt."

Which just pissed me off even more. "That won't work either," I said. "Do you want our clothes or not?" Trouble squirmed in my arms, clearly wanting another try at Little.

My dad watched me, not sure how to handle his own daughter talking back to the police.

Norma gave a sigh, as if disappointed in my behavior. She had a lot of tricks in that cop bag. "Could you put your cat somewhere while we talk?"

I locked Trouble in the downstairs bathroom, where she meowed loudly about the interlopers in her domain.

Norma explained the process to us, including that she'd have to be present while I undressed to take my clothes and shoes, while Little stayed with my dad. Talk about awkward. I guess Little following me to my bedroom would be even worse.

My dad led Little to the downstairs guest room, where he'd been sleeping since he got sick. Norma escorted me up the stairs past a wide-eyed Elliott who was perched on the landing, his favorite spying location. "It'll be okay," I told him, trying to sound reassuring. "Go back to your room."

Norma put my clothes in a large evidence bag, just like on a crime show. "Colbie," she said gently. "Is there a friend or neighbor you could all stay with tonight?"

"Why?" I asked.

She stayed silent.

"Cause you'll have a warrant soon, right?" I guessed.

"You probably want to leave your phones and computers here as well," she said. "So we don't have to bother you again tonight."

I stared at her, my mouth gaping open, the reality that we were her prime suspects sinking in. Then I realized that with my dad being so sick, I was her real target.

"I'm sorry," she said, but she couldn't possibly mean it. Underneath the surface politeness was a look, more like an energy, that reminded me of Trouble when she's stalking a bird. "The warrant will include all of your electronics."

I waved down the hall. "Take a look now while you can, because you're waiting outside until you get that warrant."

She took a cursory look inside each room upstairs, but nothing screamed *I killed Twila Jenkins* at her because she turned to follow me down the stairs.

"All of your investigating is going to prove that I wasn't even there when it happened, so you'd be smart to consider others," I said.

"That's my job," she replied.

I collected Elliott, grabbed the cat from the bathroom, holding on to her firmly, and explained to my dad where we were going. I matched my dad's slow pace down the stairs from the front porch while Detective Little looked around outside our house with a flashlight. We headed across the street to my dad's best friend, Annie Quinn's, house. My dad's neighborhood was usually very quiet at night, and the police activity had drawn a small group watching from a polite distance on a lawn down the street.

Just as I stepped off the curb, I heard a "Yes!" from the side of the house. Was that Detective Little?

"I'll be over in a minute," I said, handing Trouble to Elliott, who immediately protested.

"I won't be long," I said. "Pinky swear."

I held out my pinky finger, but Elliott rolled his eyes, too stressed to take part in our long-standing tradition. He took the cat and followed my dad, his shoulders hunched over with worry.

Annie opened the door as they approached. "Come in, come in, my dears," she called out. Standing at barely five foot, she radiated motherly concern.

I waited until they all went inside and then walked around the side of my dad's house. Little and Norma huddled over a white towel in an evidence bag.

"What are you doing?" I asked, and then I noticed that the towel was stained brown. "Is that blood?"

Norma stepped forward, as if shielding the bag from me. "Ms. Summers."

"That's not ours," I insisted.

"Right," Little said, disgusted. "And I'm sure someone is trying to *frame* you."

I could imagine him using finger quotes when he said the word "frame." A flicker of irritation flashed across Norma's face. "Detective," she warned.

"What?" he asked her. "You agree with her?" His disbelief was laced with obvious dislike, but this time it was directed toward his partner.

"Norma," I said with my voice shaking. "That does *not* belong to us."

Norma grabbed my arm and dragged me toward the front of the house. "Ms. Summers," she said through clenched teeth. "Please go to your neighbor's so we can do our job." She turned around.

"That's not our towel!" I called after her, but she didn't respond.

Annie must have been watching for me because she opened the door as I walked up her steps. "Oh my goodness. Your dad told me about your friend. Are those police nuts investigating you?"

"One of them might be," I said, and followed her inside.

My dad was already sitting in his favorite chair, a glass of whiskey in his hand. Elliott sat in the floral love seat, clutching Trouble to his chest.

"I'm just getting Elliott's hot cocoa," Annie said. "What would you like?"

"Cocoa sounds wonderful," I said. "Can I help?"

"Oh no," she said. "You sit right there by Elliott and I'll be out quick as a wink."

I followed her directions, sliding an arm around Elliott's shoulders. "It's going to be okay."

He put his head on my shoulder. "Pinky swear?" he whispered, holding out his pinky.

I grabbed it with my own finger. "Pinky swear," I whispered back.

Maybe he was thinking of the time one of our friends at the farmers' market had been arrested a year before. He'd been selling cookies containing pot at his booth and was caught by an undercover police officer. The arrest of a family friend had scared Elliott, even though it had been a good opportunity for some *don't-do-or-sell-drugs* parenting discussions.

I tried to speak casually. "So, Dad, did you put a towel in the garbage?"

He looked at me like I was crazy. "Of course not."

I smiled, trying for a *no-big-deal* expression, but it might have been closer to a grimace. "Elliott?"

He shook his head, his head brushing against my arm. "No. Why?"

"It's nothing." So, if none of us put a bloody towel in our garbage can, then who did?

Annie called out from the kitchen. "Colbie, you want some Bailey's in yours?"

"Really tempting," I said. "But no thanks."

"That's smart," she said, as she brought out our mugs. "Best to keep your wits about you."

Annie's home was an inviting combination of country chic mixed with fantasy art. I moved aside a statue of a half-naked mermaid to put down a coaster for Elliott. He took a sip of cocoa.

"Thanks so much for having us during this...mess," I said, gesturing across the street.

"No problem at all," she said. "I just adore your family." Then she handed me a business card. "This is my lawyer. Please call him and get advice before this goes any further."

Seeing that embossed card made me even more nervous. "Surely the police will figure out we had nothing to do with this." Even so, I reached out.

"Of course," she said as she pushed the card into my hand and then patted it. "But I've seen a lot of injustice in my days. Just call him to make me feel better, okay?"

"It's okay," my dad said. "I gotta guy."

"No," I said firmly and turned back to Annie. "I'll call him tomorrow." My dad frowned.

"You'll like him," Annie said, turning her charm on my dad. "He's from Boston too."

Annie was one of those people who didn't need much sleep to think straight and volunteered for the Sunnyside Library, Meals on Wheels, and an emergency hotline. She'd been the one who called to tell me my dad was in the hospital and convinced me to move in. And believe me, that hadn't been easy to accomplish. She could probably convince David Copperfield to reveal how he made the Statue of Liberty disappear.

It certainly helped that my boss had just warned me that the owner of the apartment building I managed was about to sell and would start using a professional property management company. He gave me a fair shake—offering me a severance package and everything. I put our stuff in storage and moved Elliot and me in with my dad until I could figure out the next step.

My dad and I had a complicated relationship even before I got knocked up when I was eighteen. My mother had died when I was very young, and he'd never seemed interested in dating someone new. He'd been so proud that I was the first in his family to attend college and could never let it go when I dropped out. It made it hard to visit longer than a couple of hours, even knowing how much he loved Elliott, and I usually left feeling like a failure.

He reached out and patted Elliott's leg. "It'll work out," he said. "Nuttin' to worry about."

Elliott smiled back, his shoulders relaxing just a bit, and I had to swallow the lump in my throat.

Chapter 4

Annie convinced my dad to take her guest room while Elliott slept on the pull-out sofa bed in her sewing room. I promised her that I'd be comfortable sleeping on the couch, but Trouble and I kept watch on the police activities in a high-backed chair turned around to see out the window. At midnight, I guessed that the warrant arrived because two women and two men arrived in a black SUV, wound crime scene tape around the whole property, and went inside.

I must have dozed, because at five in the morning, Trouble woke me by patting my cheek. The police and their crime scene tech buddies were all gone but the tape remained. I left a note for Annie and my family that Trouble and I were checking out the house and would be back soon. I locked up with her spare key and stood on the sidewalk looking at my dad's house. Trouble stopped purring for a moment, probably thinking, *"Get going! It's chilly out here, and my food is waiting."*

I stepped over the tape and was confronted by a crime scene tape sticker on the front door. It said something about it being a violation to gain access, blah, blah. Those detectives didn't know the trick of the living room window; the lock opened easily with a few jiggles, and soon I'd dumped Trouble inside, scrambled over the windowsill, and was standing in the darkened living room.

Trouble rushed to make sure her food and water bowls were still present and accounted for while I turned a light on and surveyed the damage. It could have been worse. The crime scene techs had put some of the stuff back into the drawers, but fingerprint dust was everywhere. My dad's computer was missing from his small desk, which upset me even though I knew it was going to happen.

The kitchen wasn't as bad, but they'd taken my laptop and the entire knife block. I had no idea why they'd do that—they already had the murder weapon. I shuddered at the memory.

Upstairs was chaotic. It was good that my dad wasn't much of a hoarder. They hadn't bothered to refold any of the clothes taken out of the dressers or closets. I guess it was nice that they'd piled them on the beds. I got to work on my dad's room first. Elliott might not even notice the jumble in his room. I wasn't sure how he'd live through the day without his phone or computer.

Underneath my dad's clothes were two shoeboxes, one labeled "Boston" and one labeled "Colbie." Of course, I opened my own box. It was full of photos and the first one I saw broke my heart. It was my dad holding me as a baby and the love on his face, so much younger and happier, burst from the photo.

I blamed stress and exhaustion for the sob that escaped me, and shoved the photo back in the box, and both boxes into the closet. Then I noticed my dad's guitar pushed into the corner. He hadn't played at all since we moved in. I brought it downstairs and propped it near his chair, hoping he'd pick it up and do something besides watch TV.

Then I got back to work.

* * * *

I woke up to Trouble walking on my chest while my dad's landline rang in the background. He still had a landline, as did plenty of people in Sunnyside, where a distrust of technology was considered common sense.

I tracked down a phone in my dad's room and answered.

"Finally!" Lani said. "Are you okay?" She must have heard about Twila to be this agitated.

"I'm fine." I looked at the clock radio on the nightstand. "Ten o'clock?"

"Yes!" she said. "I sent you a zillion texts. I was about to come over and pound on your door, but Piper found your dad's home number online. What the hell is going on?"

I tried to shake the wooziness from my head. "Can you come over and see if they took the crime scene sticker off the door?"

"Now that's something I never expected to hear from you," she said. "On my way." She hung up.

First coffee, I decided, and stumbled down to the kitchen, where I got the machine going while Trouble yowled, *"Feed me! I'm starving!"*

I followed her meowed orders and then woke up enough to realize I could see the front door from the kitchen window.

The sticker was gone, along with the crime scene tape.

I called Annie to let her and my family know that I was awake and to come home for breakfast. Or brunch.

Lani beat them to it, the bell on her bike announcing her arrival. I opened the door to see her bouncing the bike up onto the porch. The bright pink Schwinn cruiser with a flowered basket on front fit her to a T.

I couldn't help but smile. "Welcome to Crazytown."

"My kinda place," she said, taking off her helmet. She'd decorated it with *Art Saves Lives* stickers. Today her pink-highlighted hair was in a loose French braid, and she wore one of her own creations—a green camisole with contrasting panels of zoo animal prints and capris painted with yellow giraffes. The outfit should've looked like a hot mess, but was totally charming on her. "I need coffee and then you can tell me everything."

Lani followed me inside and I got her a small mug. Piper had told me that Lani had chronic indigestion and caffeine only made it worse, but she loved coffee so much it was hard to tell her, "*No. You can't have the elixir of the gods.*"

She knelt down to pet Trouble, who lifted her head from her bowl for a moment to greet her with a short meow. She grabbed the cup and poured creamer in it, then actually slurped. "Ah. Heaven." She tilted her head. "No one else home?"

"They slept at Annie's," I said.

She stared at me over the mug. "Okay, now spill. What the heck happened last night?"

I told her everything, from finding Twila's body to the search warrant scene with the bloody towel. She gasped at the appropriate moments but didn't ask any questions until I was done with my bizarre story.

"You're sure it was a Meowio knife?" she asked, appalled.

I nodded. "Totally."

"That *sucks*," she said. "I hadn't heard that detail. Maybe the police will keep it from the public, and it won't hurt your sales."

OMG! I hadn't even thought about that. Negative publicity could really hurt a business like mine, where so many new customers came from word of mouth. I already had that one negative SDHelp review.

"Where did that towel come from?" she asked. "The one that set off that Little policeman?"

"You make him sound the size of an action figure." I thought of all the ways I could torture a Little that size. One of them involved magnifying glasses and the sun. "It doesn't make sense." Then I remembered my run-in with the chickens. "Uh-oh. I threw my flip flops in the garbage."

"Why?"

I told her about the mess from the chicken coop.

"What does that have to do with the towel?"

"It doesn't," I said, but I'd seen enough TV shows to realize they might think I was trying to hide something.

"So how did a random towel that may or may not have blood on it get in there?" she asked.

I looked at the floor and then back to her face. "Worst-case scenario?"

She nodded.

"Worst case, that towel has Twila's blood on it," I said, fighting back a little shudder. "And we're prime suspects."

Her mouth made a little O of surprise. "How is that possible?"

"I haven't been able to think of anything else most of the night. There's only one person who would want to frame me."

Her eyes widened as she'd figured it out too. "The killer!"

I nodded, feeling weak. "I mean, logistically, it has to be. No one could plan to do all that ahead of time, especially to use my knife. It's a fluke that I went home and left my stuff there at the trade show."

"I agree," she said. "*We* know the towel was planted, so that's the only thing that makes sense."

I smiled at her absolute faith in me, despite how worried I was. "So maybe whoever did that to Twila saw my dad and me go to the, you know, scene of the crime and decided then and there to make it seem like I did it."

"Or your dad," she said.

I shook my head. "But he's never even met Twila. And he's so sick, no one could think he was strong enough."

She bit her lip.

I said the next part slowly, not wanting to admit it. "And it has to be someone who knows where we live because it was here, in the garbage can, before the police arrived."

"It's the perfect crime." She got up to pace the kitchen. "It was *your knife*. You were *there*. You discovered the *body*. The killer saw you go into the place and then drove here to leave evidence for the police to find at your house."

I stood to get myself another cup of coffee, even though my nerves were making me feel like screaming. "I'm totally screwed, aren't I?"

"No, you're not," she said. "Because you're innocent."

"That's not what Little thinks," I said.

She stopped her pacing. "You need to figure out who did it!"

I twisted up my mouth in a *yeah right* expression. "How?" I asked. "I don't have the money to hire an investigator. And what I do have I need to save for a lawyer."

She waved her hand around as if pushing aside my silly idea. "You have to look into this yourself."

I laughed, but it came out more like a snort.

"Look," she said. "You've met with all of those wacky power moms. One of them has to know something." She gasped. "One of them may have done it! I knew there was something strange about that group."

"I'm sure the police will talk to all of them," I said while my mind whirled with suspicion. Had I made it clear that I heard Bert Merritt open the door at the activity center while he was talking to my dad? Surely that was something the police could check.

Luckily, my dad and Elliott arrived, so Lani couldn't try to talk me into doing something foolish. Elliott held a bag filled with banana-nut muffins that Annie had just made. The smell from the still-warm muffins spread through the kitchen and we all avoided any talk of murder and mayhem, but I couldn't stop thinking about Twila.

I looked at my dad, still tired but joking with Elliott about who could eat more muffins.

Elliott shoved a whole muffin in his mouth.

"Oh yeah?" my dad said, and shoved a whole muffin in his mouth too.

That made Elliott laugh so hard he spit out a bunch of crumbs across the kitchen table.

"Oh yeah?" Lani said, and picked up a muffin. Then she took a tiny bite from the side, like a perfect lady.

For some reason, that made Elliott laugh harder than ever, and we all joined in.

* * * *

Since our computers and phones were in the hands of the police, Lani ran home to loan us an old laptop she'd kept as a backup. I was able to login to check my website orders. Then I researched when we'd get our stuff back from the police. Shoot. It could take months. We were lucky that they'd let us back into our home so quickly.

I brought the computer to my dad and he gestured for me to put it where his used to be. "I'm going to buy new phones," I said. "Do you want to go with me to pick yours out?"

He moved over to the small desk and started poking away at the keyboard. "Nah. I'll use the home phone for a while."

"Are you sure?" I asked. How could anyone live without a cell phone these days? "I looked it up. The police could keep them forever."

He looked at me over his glasses. "Really?" He thought for a minute, as if that might not be such a bad thing. "I'll wait a couple of days and see if I need it."

Amazing. I went upstairs to see if Elliott wanted to come with me—of course he did—and when I came down, my dad was frowning at the computer. Trouble had claimed his chair, stretching out diagonally. *This is all mine now.*

"Everything okay?" I asked.

"Yeah," he said. "Bert sent me an e-mail that his tech guy fixed the problem and I could move my money." He squinted through his glasses and poked at a few buttons.

"Did you e-mail him back and ask if he was at the activity center last night?" I asked. "Maybe he saw something."

He shook his head. "I did. He said the police already talked to him, and that he was at his office with his business partner all evening."

Damn. I was sure I'd heard the same security code. "Oh." My disappointment came through in my tone. "I guess I heard it wrong."

"Or he has the same code," he said, trying to make me feel better. "I'm putting some of this money in Elliott's college fund. The most I can do is fourteen."

I blinked. "Fourteen dollars?"

He scowled. "No. Fourteen thousand dollars."

I blinked and my mouth took a while to form a word. "You're giving Elliott fourteen thousand dollars?"

"Well, if I gave him more it could have tax implications," he said, pushing his glasses up on his nose and squinting at his computer.

"Fourteen thousand dollars?" I couldn't wrap my head around that my dad could hand over that much money. He'd retired from the local utility company after working for almost thirty years, starting as a lineman climbing poles and getting periodic promotions until he was offered a package to retire early. I'd worried that he'd be bored, but until he got sick, he'd enjoyed his part-time business as an electrician.

Something clicked and he looked up at me, a little warily. "Is that okay?"

I couldn't help the part of me that wanted to tell him I could take care of Elliott by myself. But why would I do that to Elliott? I took in the expression on my dad's face. Or do that to my dad? "Of course that's okay. It's just a lot of money."

He visibly relaxed and looked back at his computer. "What do you think it's for?"

* * * *

"You're going to be awesome!" I told Elliott as we got out of the car in front of the Sunnyside Recreation Center. The building was an odd conglomeration of a school built in the sixties with new wings added haphazardly over the decades. Trailer classrooms formed a semicircle in the back. The flowers surrounding the flag pole were already struggling to survive the heat, even though the summer had just begun.

Elliott shook his hands out, trying to get rid of some of his nerves. He was in total focus mode, whispering lyrics to himself as we walked in the front door.

My cell phone buzzed with a *break a leg* message for Elliott from Lani. Both Elliott and I had downloaded our contacts from the cloud, and I was already used to the new phone. I'd been smart, and went ahead and bought my dad one too. He'd grumbled a bit but had started using it right away.

I'd set my notifications to let me know if I received an e-mail or text, reflecting my own hyper-awareness. Annie's lawyer friend had said he would use his contacts to find out what he could. His low-key, don't panic message had made me feel both reassured and anxious, especially when he recommended that I don't talk to the police without him.

While I'd talked to the lawyer and then went about my normal routine, feeling like another shoe was sure to drop, Elliott had put aside the whole murder drama to focus on his callback. He'd memorized the song and practiced different ways to be in character a zillion times, and he'd shown me a hundred of them. I now knew every line to *Alone in the Universe*. If I heard the chorus to the song one more time, I might just scream.

Of course, this would be bad place to do that. Elliott put on his grown-up voice and told his name to the mom volunteer at the table with a typed *Registration* sign taped to the front. I was surprised that the auditions for a two-week summer camp had the same level of organization as a full production. Sunnyside Junior Theater certainly took their summer programs more seriously than Elliott's regular group.

"Summers?" she asked, and her eyes slid to me. She gave me the once-over. Normally, I'd just assume it was classic stage mom behavior, but I couldn't help but wonder if it had anything to do with the publicity over

Twila's murder. I'd spent most of Wednesday ignoring texts and calls from anyone I knew in Sunnyside. My dad had done the same, even unplugging his home phone after the umpteenth person called to make sure he was okay under the guise of gossiping about the murder.

I heard some murmuring behind me and looked over my shoulder. Two moms were staring straight at me.

Luckily, Elliott seemed oblivious to the whispers.

"We're running ahead of schedule, and since all of you Hortons are here nice and early, we'll send you in right away." The registration volunteer pointed to two boys waiting by the door to one of the meeting rooms. "You should wait with the other two Hortons." Both wore gray, and I immediately worried if Elliott should have worn elephant gray instead of his green button down shirt. Maybe dressing like the character you were trying out for worked on this director.

Too late now. He hugged me and went over to introduce himself to the two boys. One of them said, "Cool hair, dude," and they all began chattering away. I relaxed. In general, drama kids were incredibly friendly and accepting.

I eyed the available folding chairs against the wall, and sat as far away from the other women as possible. Another wave of young actors came in, three of them dressed like the Cat in the Hat, and the stage moms directed their attention to them.

A young man wearing a Sunnyside Youth Theater T-shirt came out from the meeting room. "Hortons? Time to make magic!" His enthusiasm was totally charming.

"Hey, Larry?" the registration mom called out. "Can I talk to the director for a minute?"

Larry raised his eyebrows, but made an elaborate bow and gestured for her to go in, and then turned to the waiting boys. "Horton One, Horton Two, and Horton Three. All accounted for. In you go."

Elliott turned to me and smiled. I gave him a thumbs-up and tried not to be nervous. He was very talented, but anything could happen during an audition. The registration mom came out, glanced at me, and hurried back to her post. What was that about?

The sound of very faint singing came from the meeting room, and I wished I'd seated myself closer. Two other moms were leaning forward. Maybe we should all stick our ears to the door. With a drinking glass.

After a few moments, the second boy sang and then the third. Then all three walked out, and I got to my feet.

Elliott looked like he was about to cry.

"It's okay," I said, and rushed him toward the front door.

He shrugged off the hand I put on his shoulder. "It's not okay," he said.

"Shh," I said, trying to make it sound soothing rather than keeping the others from hearing him have a meltdown. "Let's talk about it in the car."

He sat in the front seat and waited until I'd pulled onto Main Street to say, "I heard that mom talk to the director."

"The one who was handling registration?"

"Yeah," he said, his voice managing to sound nervous and resentful at the same time. "She told him that you were a suspect in a murder!"

"What?" Anger curdled in my stomach.

"And that maybe he should take that 'under consideration.'" His voice rose at the end.

It took me a minute to calm down enough to form a coherent thought. "What did he say?"

"He thanked her and kinda pointed to the door."

"Good," I said. "Maybe that was letting her know he wasn't taking her BS."

"Or maybe he agreed with her!" Elliott said, his voice becoming a wail.

"Elliott," I said. "It'll be okay. You had a one-third chance going in today, and you still have that." No matter what that witch tried to do. "It must have been hard to sing after that."

"Nope." He stuck his chin in the air. "I was great."

Pride flooded through me. "That's my boy. You can't let the morons get you down."

He looked out the window. "I don't know. If I don't get it, maybe it's because of what she said."

I had no answer to that and stayed silent as I pulled the car onto the highway headed toward the farmers' market. Elliott stared out the window, his shoulders slumped.

It was time to clear my name, pretty darn quick.

Chapter 5

The Downtown Farmers' Market was still bustling when Elliott and I arrived, and I slid into a parking spot of a departing customer. It was against the booth rental rules to park so close but maybe the manager wouldn't notice. Elliott helped to unload my boxes and display items, his good humor restored by the welcoming hello and free chocolate muffin tossed to him from the Muffin Man.

I quickly set up my backdrop, made sure my payment square was working on my phone, and stood in my lucky spot as Elliott brought a few more spare boxes of product from the car, storing them under the table.

Gypsy Sue, of Gypsy Sue's Love Potions & Oddities, walked across the aisle, ignoring a group of teen girls approaching her booth. "Where you been, girl?" she said. "The big bad manager was mighty pissed to have an empty booth."

I'd known Sue since before Elliott was born. She'd been a new volunteer in the teen mom program that had been my refuge when I'd left home. The program had given me my own apartment, a job, parenting training, and daycare. Sue had kept tabs on me over the years, and even convinced her apartment building management to hire me. She was one of my first customers, since her cat had digestive problems too. She'd talked me into selling my products at this farmers' market, somehow getting me moved to the front of the waitlist.

I started to explain about Elliott's audition but she interrupted me to yell to the girls, "Put it back, Blondie, or I'll curse your boyfriend, Jasper."

The blond girl wearing a neon orange miniskirt gave a mini-scream, pulled a small vial of oil out of her pocket, and hastily put it back on the shelf.

The other girls squealed an assortment of "How did she even see you?" "You're dating Jasper? Since when?" and an even more indignant, "You're dating MY Jasper?"

The whole thing was spooky even to me. Sue had been looking straight at me the whole time. "Do you have eyes on the back of your head?" I asked. "Like Mary Tyler Moore on that Dick Van Dyke show?"

"The one where Dick was dreaming about aliens?" she asked. "Love that show." She looked after the girls who had moved on to the next booth, remarkably unashamed of their unsuccessful shoplifting but still exclaiming over the incident. "I just know too much about human behavior."

One girl lingered behind, intrigued by Sue.

Sue took pity on her. "You got ten bucks, girl?" she called out. "I'll give you a psychic reading."

"Oh man," I said, looking around. The manager hated when Sue did that. Partly because he felt that it brought down the reputation of the market, but also because her accuracy freaked him out.

The girl came back without any hesitation, pulling a wrinkled ten dollar bill out of her pocket. The other teens didn't even notice her departure, and she didn't seem sorry to leave them.

Sue tucked the money into her own pocket and grabbed the girl's hand. "Your name starts with a 'P.' What is it?"

"Penny," she said, looking surprised.

"You're gonna fail your geometry test unless you study," Sue said.

Penny gasped and then waited for more.

"Ditch those girls," Sue said. "Some real trouble is heading their way."

Poor Penny did not like that news. "Really?"

"Don't need to be a psychic to know that, girl," Sue said, dropping her hand. "You know it in your heart."

The girl looked over her shoulder at her friends. "Yeah," she said, disappointed.

"You have another friend, really smart, who will be way better for you," Sue said. "Sit with her at lunch and your life will change."

The girl blinked and nodded.

"That's all I got for you today," Sue said. "Git going."

The girl pulled her backpack higher up on her shoulder and then left, the opposite direction of her friends.

"How do you do that?" I asked, even though I knew she wouldn't give me a real answer.

"Gypsy magic," she said. "Yo, Elliott!"

Elliott dropped the last box and gave her a hug. Except for my dad and me, Sue was the most constant person in his life, kind of like a fairy godmother in our times of need. He walked her back to her booth, telling her about his audition, and then took off to visit his other friends at the market.

A group of four women came up to my booth, chuckling over the coffee mugs with a cartoon of Trouble in a chef's hat on them. They carried mats and had the relaxed expressions of a recently completed yoga class.

One of them bought a ton of my Fish Romance food, fawning over the kissing cartoon fish on the label, while the other non-cat owners bought enough mugs that I could almost pay the market fee for that day.

Sue waited for them to leave before calling across from her booth, "I see you got your own trouble brewing."

I jolted in surprise. "Now that's just creepy."

She walked a few steps toward me and turned her phone around to show an article with a photo of the police at the activity center and the headline screaming, "Police Question Person of Interest in Local Murder."

* * * *

I could tell that Elliott was still worrying about the nasty volunteer mom at the audition when we packed up and left the market. I debated telling him about the article and wimped out, saying, "Whatever happens or whatever anyone says, you know that I didn't hurt Twila. We've been through some tough times and we always made it, right? This is just another tough time."

He straightened in his seat and nodded. "It's just a summer camp," he said. "It'll be fun even if I'm in the ensemble." He escaped to his room as soon as we got home.

Trouble meowed but waited for me by the living room doorway, as if wanting me to come over. For a second, I worried that she'd brought me a present—the kind that only cats would think of. But she wasn't standing over any dead rodents, so I picked her up as I walked by.

My dad was asleep in his chair, the TV blaring a commercial for some drug in spite of its many and varied side effects. A half-eaten bowl of soup sat on the side table. His breathing seemed more labored.

"Dad?" I asked.

He jolted awake and stared at me for a moment.

"You okay?"

He cleared his throat and started coughing, automatically reaching for his glass of whiskey on the side table.

"Maybe we should get you back to the doctor," I said.

He shook his head and croaked out, "I just need to rest."

I bit my lip, wondering how much to push it. He'd always been stubborn—not just about his health—and part of me thought he'd live forever. He was only sixty-two, but this pneumonia had taken a toll on him and he seemed ten years older. I wanted my healthy dad back. "I have time tomorrow if you want to get another x-ray," I tried.

He scowled. "Sometimes it just takes a while for the antibiotics to kick in." He turned the TV volume up.

Then I noticed the guitar leaning against the wall. He'd taken it out of the case. "Cool! Did you get a chance to play the guitar? How does she sound?"

"Good," he said, leaning back into the seat. "Just had to tune her up and she was fine." He stretched out his hand. "Fingers don't move as fast as they used to."

"I remember you used to play 'Puff the Magic Dragon' for me when I couldn't sleep," I said, a warm emotion tightening my throat. "I always sang that to Elliott when he had trouble sleeping."

He stared at me, surprised.

Then I had an idea. "Maybe you could teach Elliott a little guitar." My dad had tried to teach me when I was a kid, but I'd been hopeless.

He nodded. "I could do that."

"Want me to ask him?"

He paused, taking some kind of internal inventory. "How about tomorrow? I usually feel better earlier in the day."

"Makes sense." I took Trouble upstairs and dropped her in Elliott's room.

He was stretched out on his bed, holding a book that had a bloody eyeball on the cover.

"Thanks for your help at the market," I said.

He murmured, "No prob," absorbed in his book.

"Hey, you know how you always wanted to learn an instrument?" I asked him. "Maybe you should ask Grandpa to teach you how to play guitar. He's really good."

That got his attention. "Really?" he asked. "Do you think he'd want to?"

"I think he'd like it," I said.

"Now?"

He looked so excited that I felt bad disappointing him. "Grandpa's pretty tired. How about tomorrow?"

He shrugged. "Sure."

I dialed Lani and she answered on the first ring. "Did you figure out whodunit?" she asked, totally not kidding.

"No." I closed the door and plopped down on my bed. "But I'm going to."

She squealed, right in my ear. "What changed your mind?"

I told her about the stage mom at the callbacks.

She was suitably appalled. "That's nasty. I bet her son was one of the other Hortons."

Whoa. "I hadn't thought of that." Then I told her about the article.

"What?" She sounded horrified. "Hold on."

I heard her clicking away on her computer and closed my eyes to wait while she read it.

"Okay," she said. "This clinches it. You have to take control of the situation. You have the contacts. And you'll feel better than waiting around for the police to figure out who killed your friend. Let's make a list of possible suspects right now."

The bed began to feel far too comfy, as the stress of the long day caught up to me. I switched to speaker and put the phone on my stomach. "I don't think I have actual suspects yet."

She ignored me and typed away on her computer. "Everyone in your crazy mom club had the means—your knife—and the opportunity. Let's figure out who had a motive. What are all their names?"

I sighed, knowing she'd bulldoze right over me.

"Who's the slutty one?" she asked.

That woke me up. "What?"

"That mom who runs those adult parties," she said.

"Mona," I said, regretting everything I'd told Lani about the SPM members. "She's not slutty just because she sells lingerie."

"And sex toys. But you're right," she said. "I shouldn't judge. It's one of my worst traits." She typed. "Any motive?"

I sat up, trying to gather my thoughts. "Not anything having to do with Twila. But I've heard rumors that Mona…"

"Sleeps with married men," Lani finished for me.

"Do I tell you everything?" I asked.

"Yes," she said. "We're BFFs."

"And you're twelve years old," I said.

She ignored the pretend insult. "Maybe someone confused Twila for Mona."

I laughed. "They couldn't look more different from each other. Twila is, was, cute with red curly hair. Mona is tall and sexy with dark hair to her waist."

"Tell me about the rest of them," she said.

I tried to dredge up the little I knew about each one. "Gina is the one who runs those Mommy and Me classes. She's certainly strong enough to…"

"Knife someone through the chest?" Lani asked matter-of-factly. "Suspect Number One."

"I can't imagine any motive she'd have," I said.

"That's what you need to find out." She went on. "Who are the others?"

Trouble meowed at the door. I groaned as I got out of bed and opened the door for her. She came into the room and jumped on the bed, beating me back to my spot. I pushed her aside, and she settled for cuddling up beside me. "Sharon is the one who organizes closets," I said. "The closets in her brochures are so neat, they're like works of art."

"Anyone who is that organized has to have deep psychological issues," Lani said, only partly joking. "She's on the list."

I laughed. "Daria sells those BeesWax candles."

"Her prices are criminal," she said. "You have to find out what else she could be up to."

"Lani," I said, trying to calm her down.

"What about the closet woman's husband?" Lani said. "Didn't you think he was there?"

"I told the police that," I said. "But my dad talked to him and he was with his partner that night."

"I'm adding him too," she said. "Who else was at your little trade show?"

"You know Fawn," I said. "She was marketing her life coach business and raising money for her nonprofit."

"I can't imagine Fawn murdering anyone," she said. "But I know we have to keep her on the list."

"Bronx Innis," I said. "She runs that mobile dog grooming business."

"The redneck?" Lani asked.

"She's not a redneck!" I said. "She just has a southern accent."

"A southerner named Bronx," she said in a shake-your-head tone. "She's probably the only one, ever."

"Well, she likes to tell people her mom got drunk one night while visiting New York, and the Bronx is where she was conceived."

"Another one with issues," she said. "Who else?"

I made her happy by listing all the moms who were at the event, including the ones selling Tupperware, gourmet chef supplies, and inexpensive jewelry. Nothing made me think any of them could be capable of murder.

"You should invite that SPM group to your house for a meeting, but what you're really doing is interrogating them," Lani said, her voice growing excited. "You should put your notebook down at the head of the table, so they get the message that you're in control."

"Why would I want to do that?" I asked. "I don't have the time, or patience, to run that group."

"In control of the *meeting*," she said. "Heaven forbid you actually take over. Then you can ask questions from a position of authority."

"If anyone thinks I'm investigating, they won't answer questions," I said. "I think I should lie low."

"Hmm." She stayed quiet for a minute. "That's a good point. But seeing them all together could help you figure out if any of them could be the killer."

* * * *

Talking with Lani about the Sunnyside Power Moms made me realize that I hadn't even tried to get beyond a surface level relationship with any of them except Twila. I'd reluctantly joined the SPM Facebook page—when Twila requested it a second time—but other than posting information about my cat food products, I didn't spend a lot of time reading their news.

And really, we had a lot in common. We were all moms, working hard to build businesses to make a better life for our kids. I'd enjoyed our discussions about our businesses when we had meetings but I'd never tried to dig deeper.

Maybe because I assumed Elliott and I wouldn't be in Sunnyside long. Although we were taking it day by day, in the back of my mind I thought that in September, Elliott would be back at his regular school. It was a magnet school that emphasized creative and performing arts, which was a perfect fit for him.

And now wasn't the time to become friends with my fellow SPM-ers. In reality, I had to think of them all as suspects.

I went downstairs to make a quick and easy dinner, allowing Elliott to eat in his room and bringing the tomato soup and grilled cheese sandwiches into the living room so my dad and I could eat in front of the TV. "Would you mind if I asked the Sunnyside Power Moms to meet here?" I asked.

He stared at me, mouth slightly open.

"What?" I asked.

"You hardly ever brought your friends here," he said.

"They're not my friends," I said, feeling oddly defensive. "They're professional acquaintances." My dad and I had moved into this house when I was fourteen, too rebellious to realize how good I had it, and I rarely brought friends home.

"Sure," he said. "No problem. Then he grinned, like a parent finding out his kid is suddenly popular.

"It's not a playdate, Dad," I said.

My exasperation didn't dim his smile.

"Hey," he said. "I got a call from one of my buddies."

My dad had lived in Sunnyside so long that he knew just about everyone. He had a network that rivaled Homeland Security, except his was filled with his "guys." I'd quickly learned that anytime I stopped at the grocery store, or library, or Chubby's Pizza, someone was sure to ask me how my dad was feeling and how I was enjoying Sunnyside.

"He knows the sheriff's deputy. They're cousins of some kind. Anyway, he wanted to let me know that a bunch of those deputies don't think you did, you know, it."

"Really?" My voice sounded way too hopeful. "What about Norma?"

"Yeah, well, that's the tricky part," he said. "She's not telling anyone anything. She's like that, he said. Keeps her thoughts close."

"Did he say anything about Little?"

He snorted. "I don't think anyone takes him too seriously."

My cell phone buzzed, notifying me of a message. It was a group text from Daria Valdez, inviting everyone to an emergency meeting in one hour.

Even me. I couldn't help the wave of happiness that I was still included, although it didn't quite beat out the ominous feeling that I'd have to face them all.

And was she trying to take control of the group, just like Lani tried to get me to do?

* * * *

"Help me," I said to Lani. "I'm on my way to an emergency SPM meeting." A murky fog had rushed in right at sunset, forcing me to drive slowly through the streets of Sunnyside to Daria's house. The phone glowed from its stand on my dashboard.

"You didn't call the meeting?" She sounded distracted. I heard the whirring sound of her sewing machine through the phone.

"No," I answered, "Daria beat me to it. She sent a text and invited everyone to her house."

The machine stopped. "Hmm," she said. "This is better, actually."

"What do you mean?" I was surprised. "You said I should take control of the meeting, and all that."

"This way you can be sneakier," she said. "I mean, stealthy, with your questions."

"I don't even know what questions to ask," I said. "And maybe they'll be freaked out to see me." I started driving even slower, tempted to turn around and go home.

"Oh yeah," she said. "Because you found her."

"And because I'm a prime suspect," I said flatly. "Maybe I shouldn't go." I really hoped Sharon wasn't there, since I'd basically told the police her husband was at the scene of the crime.

"Let's think it through," Lani said. "You don't want them to know you're looking into it. Then you'll never get information from anyone," she said, echoing what I had said to her last night.

"This is going to be awful," I said. How was I going to face so many women who were not only sad about the loss of their friend, but might believe I had something to do with her murder.

"You'll be fine," she said, trying to sound reassuring. "More than fine. You'll be excellent. You'll be the greatest sleuth since Miss Marple."

"She was fictional," I said.

Lani ignored that and went into even greater rah-rah mode. "Okay, so first you let them know that you were very grateful for Twila's friendship and regardless of what they might have heard, you had no reason to hurt her. And that you're even more thankful for your professional relationship with them. Oh! *And* you really appreciate all of those who reached out to you to offer support."

"No one has done that." Which made me a little mad. Why hadn't at least one of them contacted me?

"I know," she said "That will make them all feel guilty for not being more sensitive. Then add something about the community you've all created, blah, blah."

"And why am I saying all that?" I asked.

"To get them on your side. You have to remind them that you're part of their team, and maybe they'll reveal their secrets," she said patiently as if talking to a child. "The conversation will surely turn to Twila anyway. See if you can get them to start speculating about who killed her. Remember who says what. And go from there."

She made it seem easy.

I pulled up in front of Daria's house, watching wisps of fog drift by the streetlamp. Her home was a clone of my dad's but with a larger front lawn. I wasn't ready to get off the phone, but then Gina pulled up behind me in her red Jeep. "Okay, one of them has seen me. I have to hang up."

"Break a leg, I mean, good luck!" Lani said.

I took a deep breath and got out of my car before joining Gina to walk toward the front porch. She'd changed out of exercise clothes into a cute sundress with a short-sleeved shrug that showed off her toned arms.

"This is just terrible," I said.

"It's the worst," she agreed, looking uncertain.

My phone buzzed in my pocket. Behind her back, I pulled it out to see a text from Lani. *On second thought, see if anyone is trying to take over the group. Possible motive!*

I almost laughed out loud. Twila volunteered to run the group only because no one else wanted to do the work.

The front door was propped open and we could hear a hum of conversation coming from the kitchen. I peeked into the dining room and saw a notebook at the head of the table. I moved closer and saw a BeesWax Parties logo of a bee holding a flaming candle on it. Daria and Lani must have learned the same take control tactics. But why would Daria want to be in charge?

Gina had gone ahead, joining everyone in the kitchen. I bit my lip and moved in, hovering right inside the doorway.

The conversation stopped.

Chapter 6

My heart started racing, and I waited in nervous silence until Daria stepped forward. "Hi Colbie. Can I get you a glass of wine? Chardonnay? Pinot?" She was wearing all black except for short purple boots.

"Um, anything's good. Thank you," I said. Then I pushed my shoulders back. I trusted Lani's people sense. I'd use her words and win them over. "Can I just talk about the elephant in the room? I want you all to know that I didn't do it. Twila was my first friend here after I moved to Sunnyside, and I was very grateful that she brought me into this group. I would never hurt her. I know that the police will clear me. I know it, simply because I didn't do it."

I paused and took turns looking each of them in the eye as I added, "I value our professional relationships and friendships that we've built, and I'm really grateful to all of you who reached out to me in the last couple of days. I hope that this horrible act doesn't hurt the important work that we do together."

I knew that was going a little over the top, but everyone seemed to relax. Perhaps it had worked.

Daria was the first to step forward. "Of course not," she said, and gave me a hug.

Tears unexpectedly threatened and I hugged her back, holding on a bit too long.

She dropped her arms and stepped back, looking a little weepy herself. "Definitely time for that wine."

The others moved forward with hugs, pats on the arm, and murmurs of "It'll be okay," and "We'll get through this together."

Sharon was the last one. Before she could say anything, I said, "I'm so sorry for the misunderstanding." That was a nice euphemism for *telling the police your husband was at the scene of the crime.*

I had interrupted whatever she was going to say because she paused with her mouth open. She closed it and said, "It's okay, dear. You were under a great deal of stress, finding her and all. And that's been cleared up." She patted my shoulder in a *there-there* gesture.

Daria delivered a large wineglass practically filled to the top with chardonnay. I grabbed it dramatically with both hands. "I definitely need some of that."

The others laughed more than the joke deserved, and the tension in the room dropped even more. Daria touched my arm and walked me over to the appetizers, allowing the others to move into small groups. Even though I wasn't hungry, I grabbed a few grapes and slices of cheese.

The beginning of our meetings was usually somewhat social with everyone asking each other about families. When I first joined, this was the most painful part of the meetings. These moms had known each other for years and knew enough to talk about families, their kids' teachers, tryouts for various teams, and the politics involved with getting the best coach. They were starting from scratch with me, asking if I had children and what my husband did. Only Twila had gone deeper—asking what Elliott was into and why I'd chosen to sell cat food.

I'd held back, believing I wouldn't be in Sunnyside long enough to learn much about this group of suburban moms, let alone fit in. But being here now made me realize I'd quickly become so entangled in this group that I knew Daria's daughter had made the junior varsity cheerleading squad and had to decide between that and gymnastics, that Bronx's husband lost his IT job and was driving for Uber, and that Fawn had recently been forced to buy condoms for her eighty-five-year-old grandmother-in-law who was having way too good of a time at the retirement community she'd never wanted to move to.

I wouldn't say I was friends with them, but I was further down the friends path than I thought.

Daria realized that we were running out of small talk and suggested, "Should we move into the dining room?"

Everyone was being ultra-polite to everyone else and to avoid more awkward "after you" exchanges, I grabbed the first seat that wasn't at the other end of the table from Daria. No way did I want to look like I was challenging anyone for an upgrade in my pecking order. Everyone else avoided that seat too. Smart ladies.

Daria had fit as many of her products as she could into her dining room décor. A complicated dining table centerpiece held coconut-smelling tea lights, trios of pillar candles sat on the display shelf against the wall, and ornate wall sconces held long taper candles.

"I called this meeting so we could figure out what to do," Daria said, looking serious. "We all loved Twila." She paused to clear her throat, emotion getting the best of her. "I've had individual talks with a few of you, and I want to make sure we have a consensus to continue this group."

Everyone nodded as she looked around the room.

"I'm willing to coordinate," she said. "I won't be as good as Twila, but I'll do my best."

"You'll do fine," Mona said, while everybody added their support, too.

The rest of the meeting went smoothly, with other moms agreeing that our next event should coincide with Sunnyside's Halloween Festival, followed by a Holiday Fair in early December. I didn't know if I'd still be here then, but went along with the crowd.

Daria let everyone know that she'd lead the group through the next school year, and that someone else would have to step up after that. Everyone gratefully accepted, totally assuming the *someone else* wouldn't be them. I'd bet ten-to-one that poor Daria would be in charge far longer than she assumed.

Fawn spoke up, her voice tentative. "I've noticed a spike in visits to the SPM website, especially Twila's puzzle site. I'm still her website administrator. You all have links there—are you seeing more activity?" Fawn had designed the group website along with many of the members' sites.

Mona nodded. "I'm not sure if it's because of the trade show or..." Her voice trailed off.

"Is anyone else getting more orders this week?" Daria asked.

A few nodded.

Shoot. I wasn't.

"That's just...wrong," Fawn said.

* * * *

Stay after and see what the candle lady is up to.

Following Lani's texted order, I lingered after the meeting, helping Daria with clean-up long past the other moms, who had listened to her saying she'd handle it and left.

"I just wanted to thank you for including me," I told Daria once we were alone in the kitchen. "I know you must have thought twice about it, and I understand. I'd worry about the same thing in your situation. So thanks."

"What happened to Twila is a tragedy," she said, while loading small plates in the dishwasher. "We have to work together to get past it."

"You're going to be a wonderful leader." I took my time washing a wineglass in hot, soapy water while watching her out of the corner of my eye. "I just can't imagine why anyone would want to hurt Twila."

She shook her head. "It doesn't make any sense."

"She seemed to get along fine with all of the moms," I said.

A thoughtful expression crossed her face.

"What?" I asked. "Did any of them give her trouble?"

"Not really," she said, reluctant to answer.

I tried to figure out how to get her to reveal more without outright asking. "I can't imagine any of the moms having a problem with how she organized us. I hope they won't give *you* a hard time."

"Nothing like that," she said. "Twila just mentioned last week that she felt like one of the members was doing something...."

"Something what?" I kept my tone light, which was difficult.

"Like, unethical." She frowned.

Unethical?

"That's weird," I said as if I couldn't believe it. "I don't know everyone as well as you do, but does anyone seem like they'd be unethical?"

She waved her hand around as if wanting to dismiss the whole thing. "Yeah. That couldn't be true."

I remembered her fight at the trade show. "Any chance it was Mona?"

Her face darkened. "I asked Twila, but she said it wasn't her. And then she changed the subject."

"But she didn't tell you who?" I asked, holding my breath.

She shrugged. "Nope."

I couldn't help but wonder. What could one of us do that Twila would think was unethical? And did it lead to her murder?

* * * *

I arrived at home to see an unfamiliar car in the driveway and went inside to see a man I didn't know sitting with my dad. "Hey, Colbie," my dad said. "I'd like you to meet Bert, my financial guy."

Oh man. I felt a wave of embarrassment. I'd practically accused him of murder. "Nice to meet you," I said. "Can I offer you anything to drink?"

"I'm good," he said. "Thanks." He was a slightly overweight man in his fifties, with salt and pepper hair. He was wearing a suit and tie. Even in our air conditioning, he had to be uncomfortable.

I stayed in the doorway. "Dad, you want anything?"

He shook his head and lifted his glass. "Bert brought me my favorite whiskey."

"How nice," I said. "Is Elliott upstairs?"

"Yeah," my dad said. "Your cat wasn't happy about my guest." He used that disapproving tone of voice that drove me crazy as a teen.

"Oh, sorry," I said. "She's still getting used to being here."

"I'll get out of your hair." Bert stood up. "I just stopped by to see one of my favorite clients." He sent my dad a warm smile. "Even though he did practically clean out his account."

"Life happens," my dad said, unapologetically.

"When you're back on your feet, you can take another look and see if you want to keep getting that awesome return," Bert said, as enthusiastic as a puppy. He tugged at his tie.

"I'll do that," my dad said. "Say hello to your lovely wife."

"I will." He shook my dad's hand. "You feel better, okay?"

I walked him to the door. "Your dad says your business is thriving." He smiled. "A proud papa, he is."

"Aw," I said. "That's nice to hear."

He continued. "Feel free to let me know if you need any investment advice, okay?"

"Of course," I said. "But right now, I'm putting all the profits back into the business."

He nodded. "Smart, smart."

"I hope so," I said.

He must have heard something in my voice. "Sorry. Can't always turn off the sales guy inside."

"I get it," I said.

"Hank's looking much better," Bert said. "He's lucky to have you to take care of him."

* * * *

Early the next morning, I was back in the kitchen making a pot of coffee before the sun was up. A couple of hours and a few packed boxes ready to ship later, my dad was sitting under the umbrella on the back deck with his coffee, waiting patiently for Elliott to wake up. The temperature was rising quickly, and he'd be forced inside soon.

Elliott had been up late hoping for the cast list to be posted, but at midnight someone had updated the Sunnyside Youth Theater site to say it would be on the website at noon today.

The doorbell rang out "Yankee Doodle" and my shoulders tensed. The police again?

I peeked out the side window and saw Charlie's silly crown. I relaxed.

Stripping off my gloves, I yelled out to my dad, "I'm taking Charlie back."

Charlie waited on the porch, tilting his head as if to ask me why I wasn't inviting him in.

"Time to go home," I said.

When the bird didn't move, I added in a sympathetic tone, "I know. You're born to be a rolling stone but doomed to captivity." I bent over to steer the bird down the stairs with gentle pushes, and he moved along.

I straightened as soon as he headed in the right direction, and we made it back to the farm with no problem. Then I had a decision to make. Put the bird back into his pen or pretend ignorance and knock on the door so I could get another look at my cute neighbor?

The decision was made for me when Joss came out of a distant small building, wearing a gray tank top and carrying a bale of hay by its strings. The strings were probably called something else in farmer language, but my brain sputtered at the sight of his flexed arms. His muscles were shining, like the cover of a romance novel.

Of course, it was already eighty degrees at eight o'clock in the morning, something that rarely happened in downtown San Diego, but was becoming normal for me here in Sunnyside. I was sweating quite a bit myself, but not in an artistic, front of the shirt emphasizing chest muscles way like Joss. My sweating was more of the eye makeup-smudging, shiny forehead, wet under-boob way.

He smiled as he recognized me. "We have to stop meeting like this," he called out.

I pointed to Charlie. "Blame the chicken."

He dumped the hay bale by the chicken coop and opened the gate near me. "How's your dad?" he asked, as he bent over to pick up Charlie and tuck him under one arm.

Charlie leaned his head on his shoulder.

I was oddly touched by the chicken hug. "He was doing better, but his cough has kicked up again."

"He's strong," he said, absentmindedly petting Charlie's head.

"Feel free to stop by and visit him," I said. "If you have time, that is." Geez. Did it sound like I was using my dad's illness as an excuse to invite him over?

He paused. Was he wondering the same thing or thinking of his farmer To Do list. "I'll stop over in an hour or so," he said. "If that's okay."

"Perfect," I said. "I'll put more coffee on."

"Sounds good," he said, and opened the gate to deposit Charlie back in his pen.

I walked back toward home, dripping even more in the bright sun and totally lost in my own thoughts. Then I heard a voice coming from the house a few doors down from my dad's. "Saw you had some trouble the other night."

I shielded my eyes from the sun sneaking in around my sunglasses, and peered at the porch that was in shadows. "Hello?"

An older man with long gray hair pulled back into a ponytail leaned his hip on the wooden railing. "Your boy get into trouble? He's at that age."

I gasped. "No!" I struggled to control my anger that someone would falsely accuse my kid like that. He didn't even know him.

But this was my dad's neighbor. Maybe being a jerk was his way of showing concern. "I'm sorry. I don't think we've met. I'm Colbie Summers."

"I know who you are," he said snidely, as if he was one up on me. "I'm Horace."

"It's nothing that won't be cleared up soon," I said. "Have a good day." It was delivered a little more savagely than most people said it.

Chapter 7

I seethed the rest of the way home.

"Judgmental jerk," I said out loud and, too late, saw Detective Norma Chiron sitting in a dark blue car outside my house, watching me in her rearview mirror. I hadn't noticed her there when I left. Ugh. Her window was open. Had she heard me? And how could she stay seated in the car in this heat?

"It's kind of my job." She smiled as she got out of her car. "You know, to judge people." She wore a lightweight jacket over jeans.

Then I noticed another police officer in the car across the street. A man staring at me with reflective sunglasses. At least it wasn't Little.

"I wasn't talking about you," I said, feeling uncertain about her friendly expression.

"Sure," she said in a two syllable, sarcasm-infused way with what seemed to be a genuine smile. "I'd like to talk to you and your father."

I took a deep breath. "Sure," I said, mimicking her, and led the way to the stairs.

The other officer got out of his car.

"Who's that?" I asked.

"Detective Ragnor is backing me up today," she said.

"Detective Little too busy?" I asked. Not that I missed him.

She didn't answer. "So who was the Judgey McJudgerson?"

"You sound like my son," I said. No way was I answering her question. That was all I needed, for her to go interrogating my dad's neighbors.

"I got that one from my twelve-year-old," she said. "But daughter instead of son. They come up with the funniest expressions, don't they?"

I stopped short, one step above her. "Look," I said. "Please don't use the mom card when you're trying to get information out of me."

Her face went blank. "I apologize."

"Should I have my lawyer present?" I blustered.

She frowned. "I didn't ask you anything."

"Then why are you here?" I said.

Detective Ragnor stepped closer at my louder tone, and Norma waved him back. "This case is bothering me."

"What part?" I asked. "The grisly murder of an innocent suburban mom or the attempt to pin it on me?"

She paused. "Both, I guess." She rolled one shoulder in an impatient move. "You're not stupid."

"I like to think so," I said.

"So you wouldn't be smart enough to get rid of bloody shoes, and then drive by a dozen public garbage cans and hundreds of private ones, only to discard a towel with the victim's blood on it at your own house."

The overwhelming relief that she wasn't buying the effort to implicate me fought with her disturbing mention of "victim's blood." "Um, thanks. I guess."

She almost cracked a smile. "I get suspicious when I catch a case all wrapped up in a big ol' bow like this one. I don't like it."

"Probably about as much as I like being framed for murder," I said. Too bad my voice shook. I cleared my throat enough to ask, "Victim's blood?"

"DNA results will take a while," she said. "But I expect it will be the case."

I took a deep breath. "What do you want?"

"I'd like to find out if your father or you have any enemies," she said, pulling out a notebook from her pocket.

My mouth dropped open. "Enemies?" I stuttered. "I haven't lived here long enough to make enemies."

"I understand your previous job included evicting people," she said, all business.

"What?" Why was I surprised? Of course she'd looked into my background. "Okay. I evicted like four people in many, many years. I had the best rate of all the apartment managers in Southern California."

"Your building is not that far away," she said. "If anyone was holding a grudge."

"That makes no sense. They'd have to somehow know I was going to be at the trade show, get in and,"—I gulped—"kill Twila, and then leave the evidence at my house. And magically know that I was going to leave my Meowio knives there."

She nodded, as if she'd already come to that conclusion. "But the event was advertised on social media and had all of the participants' names listed."

I'd thought of that. It still didn't make sense for me to be the target. "It has to be the person who killed Twila. Then my dad and I came stumbling in and gave them the perfect way to deflect attention away from him and pin it on us."

"If that's true, the person had to know where you lived," she said.

"Or my father," I said. "And he knows just about everyone in Sunnyside."

She nodded, again as if she already knew that. "I'd like to take this discussion inside."

It suddenly occurred to me that she really hadn't asked any questions. Definitely a police officer ploy to keep us from calling our lawyer. Although she seemed genuine when she said we were innocent. But maybe that was another police officer trick.

I decided that our little discussion could be a two-way street, and I'd ask my own questions.

I led the way up the porch steps and inside. The air conditioning was a welcome respite from the heat outside. "Dad?" I called out, hoping his robe was closed. "Detective Chiron is here."

"Oh joy," he said. The volume of CNN in the background went down considerably.

Ragnor opened the door and stepped into the hallway. He stayed inside, right by the front door.

"It's okay," Norma told him.

"What's his problem?" I asked. "Does he think we're some kind of threat?"

"Standard practice," she said. "No one is supposed to go alone."

I waited for my dad's chair to creak, while he made himself more presentable, before we went into the living room. He surprised me by being fully dressed in real pants and a button-down shirt. Maybe he was feeling healthier.

Trouble meowed as she jumped down from my dad's lap, and then stopped to stretch sleepily. She walked toward us and I reached down to pick her up, but she slid out of my hands to weave around Norma's ankles.

Traitor.

Norma bent down to pet her, and Trouble leaned into her hand, purring.

"Can I get you some coffee, Detective?" I asked.

"That'd be great," she said. "And it's Norma."

She took one end of the couch, and Trouble jumped up to lie beside her as I headed into the kitchen.

"Coffee?" I asked Ragnor quietly.

He shook his head, expressionless.

"Brownie?" I asked.

His mouth twitched. "No, but thanks."

I moved quietly in the kitchen, all ears on what was happening in the living room.

My dad cleared his throat. "What's this about?"

"I'm just trying to clear up a few things," Norma said. "You can certainly get your lawyer here, but you don't have to answer anything."

"Cream or sugar?" I called from the kitchen, letting her know I was close enough to hear everything.

"Just cream, please," she said.

"What do you want to know?" my dad asked, then had a coughing fit. I guess he wasn't doing that much better.

"I'd like a list of people who might want to do either of you harm," she said.

"Harm?" my dad asked. "Me or my daughter? And why are you asking?"

I brought the coffee back in and took the chair on the other side of my dad.

"We're looking at all possibilities," she said.

My dad leaned forward. "I have a lot of friends in this town, including in the sheriff's department. They're saying you don't think either one of us did it."

Her face tightened. Sunnyside was a small town. What did she expect? "What I think is not relevant. I still have to follow the evidence."

He pursed his lips. "Well, I can tell you straight out that the evidence is going to prove we didn't do anything."

"We don't have any enemies," I said to Norma. "You need to find out who killed Twila and that'll be the one who tried to frame me. Not the other way around."

"We need to exhaust every option." Her voice was firm. "I need a list of the people you evicted."

"They were good people." Then I remembered someone I didn't officially evict. I bit my lip.

Norma noticed that. She noticed everything. "Who are you thinking about right now?"

I took me a moment to answer. "There was this tenant who I realized too late was a drug dealer. I was told that he gave pot to a thirteen-year-old in the complex."

"Okay," she said, encouraging me.

"My management wouldn't do anything about it without proof." I still felt angry about that.

"So what did you do?" she asked.

"Well, he got arrested a week later," I said.

"For dealing pot?" she asked.

"For dealing meth."

Her eyes hardened. Meth was an epidemic in San Diego, coming over the border in horrific amounts that were devastating whole communities.

She figured out what I did right away. "Did he know it was you who turned him in?"

I didn't answer. I'd never told anyone what I'd done.

"You turned him in?" My dad laughed, sounding like he approved.

"I didn't know about the meth," I said. "As far as I know, he has no idea. And you'd know if he was in Sunnyside," I insisted. "He looks like a drug dealer. He couldn't just hang out on some suburban street without someone noticing."

"You haven't seen all of Sunnyside." Her voice was grim. "Give me his name. I'll find out where he was incarcerated. And make sure he's still there."

"Okay," I said. "Did you talk to Bert Merritt?"

My dad made a face, not liking that I was still pointing the finger at his buddy.

"Yes," Norma said. "He has a solid alibi."

"Which is what he told me," my dad said with a *let-it-go* expression. He turned back to Norma. "I might know some folks with an ax to grind."

* * * *

After a way too long discussion about our potential, if improbable, enemies, I walked Norma outside.

Ragnor's expression may have edged into impatience.

"Shoulda had that brownie," I told him and was rewarded with an actual smile.

"So Detective Little mentioned the Wilson case," I said. "What did he mean that this was just like it?"

She frowned, maybe not liking that I was asking. Or that I heard him. Or that he said anything at all where I *could* hear it.

"I can't discuss it," she said. "But feel free to Google it. Basically, it's a case where Little was right and I was wrong."

Just then, a police car came zooming around the corner. Detective Little jumped out and stopped short when he saw the three of us.

"Detective Little," Norma said. "What are you doing here?"

"I saw the lab results," he said.

"Who is the case manager?" she said in a mild tone that held a hint of steel.

He drew his shoulders up, bristling. "You are."

"Then what are you doing?" she asked.

"I was following up," he said, undeterred.

Ragnor stepped closer to Norma, clearly backing her up.

My heart was pounding at the lethal look in Little's eye. I was dying to ask, *"What results?"* but decided to wait for a better time. Like when Little wasn't around.

He ripped his sunglasses off his face. "What the hell is going on?"

Norma took a step so that she stood in between us. "Check your phone," she said.

"What?"

"Check your phone." It was a command.

Little's face turned beet red, looking remarkably like an angry emoji head. Someone had to check that guy's blood pressure before his whole body exploded.

He looked at his phone and then glared at Norma. "What do you have on him that he cuts you so much slack?"

Her expression grew steely. "You think your uncle is the kind of guy I could have 'something on'?"

When he didn't respond, she added, "I guess you could always ask him that yourself."

He blew out a breath, and I could almost see him counting to ten in his mind. Someone's had anger management training.

"If you would get your head on straight," she began and even Little seemed to know she meant *"out of your butt."* She stopped and cleared her throat. "You have to see that only an idiot would throw away the perfect piece of evidence at their own home."

"We arrest plenty of idiots," he said.

She narrowed her eyes.

"What about the phone call?" he demanded.

Phone call?

Norma took a deep breath. "Do. Not. Discuss. This. In. Front. Of. A. Suspect."

Hey! She just said I wasn't a suspect.

His face seemed to get even more red, edging toward purple. He set his sunglasses on his face. "It looks like you've got this under control all by yourself."

We watched as he slammed his car door and drove away, a lot more sedately than he had driven in. For some reason, it felt even more threatening.

"What's his problem?" I asked, my voice cracking a bit. "Besides the fact that his brain is a lot smaller than his muscles."

When she didn't answer, I asked, "Steroids? They can cause that kind of behavior, right?"

Ragnor snorted a little and headed across the street to his car.

"Maybe his last name gave him a complex?" I asked. "That's it, right?"

"Have a good day," Norma said. Her voice was serious but her eyes were laughing as she drove away.

Chapter 8

I went over everything I could remember from the conversations with the police while cleaning up the last of the pans that had been soaking in the kitchen sink. I really wanted to ask Norma about the phone call that Little had mentioned. And what weird office politics were going on with Norma and Little? What uncle were they talking about? It was like a little police soap opera going on in my dad's small town. Although I doubted very much that Norma and Little would end up together in a future episode where good characters turned evil and evil characters turned good.

Elliott ran down the stairs. "Mom!"

It took me a split second of Mom-radar to realize he was excited and not upset. "What?"

He stopped in the doorway, beaming and breathless. "They just posted the cast list and guess who's Horton?"

I couldn't help but grin. "Who?" I asked, even though I could tell from his face.

"Me!" He ran around the house, jumping up and down and throwing his hands in the air while shouting, "Yeah!"

Trouble watched Elliott from her perch on the window sill, narrowing her eyes every time he came into the doorway. *Stop this unseemly display.*

So the comments by the registration volunteer hadn't swayed the director. Or maybe he'd decided to put her in her place. I'd been around enough youth theater groups to know that was a possibility too.

I walked into the living room to see my dad wiping away a tear. "Dad?"

"I'm okay," he said with a strained smile.

I walked over and put my hand on his shoulder. "Really?"

Elliott walked into the room, suddenly silent.

"I'm just so proud of you," he said to Elliott. "And." He stopped and cleared his throat, unleashing another wave of coughing.

I patted his back, feeling the strain of his muscles fighting the spasms.

"And glad I got to be here, you know, when you got the news." He smiled at Elliott.

"I'm glad we're here too," I said. *Where's my dad and what have they done to him?* I tried to joke to myself, but couldn't stop the wave of my own gratitude. Maybe having us live here was softening him up.

"Me too," Elliott said, sitting on the floor in front of him. "And you'll come to my shows. I mean my show. It's just summer camp so there's only one."

Someone knocked at the door. "Oops. I forgot to tell you that I invited Joss over."

Elliott jumped to his feet. "Cool!" He ran to open the door.

My dad sniffed and ran a hand over his face. "Getting old."

"You look fine," I said. "Want some coffee?"

"Sure," he said. "That'd be great."

Elliott was only slightly less enthusiastic telling Joss the news. I could hear the slap of their high five from the living room.

Joss came in and gave my dad a hearty handshake, putting his hand on his shoulder. "Hiya, Hank," he said. "You're looking good." He'd showered and changed into a tight, black T-shirt, and the scent of manly soap wafted by. Then he turned those blue eyes on me. "He's doing better, right?"

"I'm getting there," my dad answered for me. Then he coughed and reached for his glass of water. "Slowly."

"Hmm," Joss said, and sat on the couch. Trouble decided to join us and slid around Joss's ankles before hopping onto my dad's lap. Watching Joss must be more interesting than watching birds. Joss leaned back into the couch cushions with a sigh and his shirt tightened across his chest. I had to agree with Trouble.

"Coffee?" I asked him.

"That'd be great," he said.

"Cream? Sugar?"

"A lot of both," he said with a smile and then turned to my dad. "The chicks miss you."

I decided not to make the obvious joke and went into the kitchen.

"They must be getting big," my dad said with a wistful tone.

"You'll have to get better fast so you can see them soon," Joss said.

"Working on it," he said. "I guess you heard about the trouble."

I almost dropped the mugs. What was he doing? Directing the subject away from his health by talking about being a murder suspect? Maybe he thought it was an elephant in the room or something and was trying to get it discussed so he could move on to other things.

"Yeah," Joss said, sounding uncomfortable. "Horace said something about the police being here."

My dad nodded. "Yeah. One of them was a piece of work."

I rushed to deliver the mugs of coffee. "Joss doesn't want to hear about that," I said, trying to sound upbeat and cheerful instead of like I was shutting him up. I handed one to my dad first and then Joss.

He reached out and our hands touched. Whoa. I felt a weird spark and almost dropped the coffee. "Sorry," I said and met his eyes. Maybe it had been too long since I'd been this close to a cute guy.

He looked a little surprised. Had he felt something too? Or was he just worried that I'd almost dumped hot coffee on him?

It had been a very long time since I'd been attracted to someone. I sat on the opposite end of the couch from him, wondering what I should do about it. If anything—I so did not need that complication right now. Then he leaned forward to put his mug on a coaster and something in the way he moved got me again. Okay, maybe I could add one more complication to my life.

Unfortunately, my dad brought me back to earth. "That poor woman," he said. "You probably heard we found her."

Oh man. Now it was a woolly mammoth in the room.

Joss's eyebrows rose. No, he hadn't heard.

"Dad," I said. "Joss doesn't want to hear about that."

"Sure he does, sure he does," my dad said and coughed.

"Did you take your medicine?" I asked.

More coughs. "I'm fine." He cleared his throat. "Where was I?"

I had to put an end to it. "We went back to the little trade show where I was selling my cat food, and we found her…body. We called the police, who questioned us because we were there. It's over."

My dad blinked at me and he shut up. Maybe he finally realized I didn't want the matter discussed.

"Sounds very upsetting," Joss said, sitting back further into the couch.

"It was. It still is," I said.

"Especially because they're treating us like suspects," my dad said.

For the love of—

Elliott had been watching us all talk, his head swinging back and forth like he was at a tennis match. He must have sensed my tension because he changed the subject. "I'll have a lot of solos in the play," he said. "Hey, you should come and see me!"

Joss smiled. "Maybe I will."

The rest of the conversation was light, until Joss finished his coffee.

"You're welcome to stay for a pizza and ice cream celebration lunch," I told him.

"Wish I could," he said. "But lots to do back home."

Elliott jumped to his feet to follow him to the door, beating me by seconds. "You should bring your daughter to the play," Elliott said. "She'll like it."

Joss stood. "Sounds like a great idea."

Daughter?

* * * *

We had a nice celebration with my dad insisting on coming to the kitchen table. He was still hunched over, but had enough energy to listen to Elliott talk more about the play. Elliott ate half the pizza himself.

I couldn't get the police visit out of my mind. "Hey, Dad. Do you have any idea what the problem between Little and Norma is?"

"Sure," he said. "Little's uncle is the sheriff, the head honcho. Little thinks that means he should get special favors. But he's such a bozo that his uncle keeps his distance. Which makes him a pain in the ass for everyone."

Elliot spooned up the last of his ice cream. "Hey, Grandpa, can you teach me how to play guitar?"

My dad looked pleased. "Sure. Let's go back to the living room and we'll start with tuning."

When Elliott looked disappointed, he added, "And then we'll get into the fun stuff."

I cleaned up the kitchen, catching a little bit of the lesson. A half hour later, Elliott came in. "Grandpa's a little tired, and I have a bunch of lines to memorize before Monday."

"Already?" I asked.

"Yeah," Elliott said. "We're putting on a full musical in *two weeks.*"

"Go for it, kid," I said. I checked on my dad and he was napping in his chair. I couldn't believe he hadn't told me that Joss had a daughter. I'd have to ask him about it another time.

Seeing Joss's reaction to the news about Twila left me feeling antsy, so I pulled up the list of potential suspects Lani had made.

I really should talk to each of the Sunnyside Power Moms individually to find out what they knew. The hard part was making sure they didn't realize I was questioning them. I hoped to run into each one of them in the normal course of their lives, but it would take time to figure out how.

And how much research could I do before it trickled over into stalking? Besides, I had cat food to make, and a dad and kid to take care of.

Gina's schedule was online and I saw that I could make it to the park by the end of one of her Mommy and Me exercise classes. I let Elliott know I'd be out, and to keep an eye on his grandfather. I pulled into the parking lot just as Gina and a pack of thirteen other mothers pushing jogging strollers circled the outside of the park and stopped at the picnic benches with "Reserved for Mommy and Me Class" signs taped to them.

Most of them bent over, panting and grabbing at their water bottles. A few had to deal with disgruntled children, but Gina's baby gurgled happily while Gina jogged in place and expertly moved the stroller back and forth.

I couldn't hear what she said, but her class went into cool down and stretch routine. I tried to remember the last time I'd done anything but jog on my dad's ancient treadmill and thought longingly of my gym in the city. Maybe I could fit in a few exercise classes around my farmers' market schedule.

When only a few of her clients remained, I got out of my car with a bag of cat food as a prop. "Hey, Gina, you teach your classes here?" I asked. "I'm meeting a customer for a special delivery."

She frowned as if not quite believing me, so I switched my bag to my other hand, letting it fall open a bit to show her the cat food inside. "What a cutie!" I said and made a funny face at her baby, eliciting a delighted giggle. "You're just a doll, aren't you?"

Gina relaxed. No mom could resist someone gushing over their kid.

"What's her name?" Even though she was dressed in green, I remembered that she was a girl. The pink unicorn toy was a clue as well.

"Joyce," she said, smiling down at her.

"I'm so glad I ran into you," I said. "I'm trying to get past what happened but I have so many questions."

"Like what?" she asked.

"I didn't know Twila very well," I said. "Could you tell me anything about her?"

"I guess." She looked at her watch. "But you'll have to run with me."

"What?" My plans didn't involve calisthenics.

"My next class is in ten minutes at the Wycomb Park," she said. "I need to run over there."

"Um," I said, looking down at my flip flops. "I only have twenty minutes before my customer gets here."

"Plenty of time to run there and back," she said and then scowled at my shoes. "Do you know how unhealthy those things are? Besides the fact that they slow you down considerably, they kill your heel. And most people don't know this but they really mess with your posture 'cause your toes are working so hard to hold them on. Do you have any other shoes in your car?"

I thought about the ratty Converse sneakers in the trunk. "Yes, hold on."

She waited impatiently, and I realized she was always impatient. "What do you want to know?"

I dropped the bag on the back seat of the car and put my shoes on.

She frowned at my lack of socks, but didn't say anything.

"I'm just trying to…come to terms with Twila's death." I put on my sad face, which wasn't too far away when I thought about her. "She was so nice. Like, do you know *anyone* who didn't like her?"

She started jogging in place and looked toward the other side of the park as if estimating how long it would take her to get there.

"Everyone liked her," she said. "That's why I think it was random, or a robbery or something."

I took a deep breath. "A robbery at a little thing like that?"

"Ready?" she asked, and started running.

I fell into step with her, my muscles feeling stiff and awkward. I really needed to find time to exercise. Gina was almost a decade older than me and I was already huffing while she breathed easily as she pushed the baby stroller. And that was after running an exercise class.

"So," I puffed out. "You really think a stranger could get into a gated community like that?"

She waved her hand in a dismissive gesture. "The gate was propped open for the two hours of the event."

"Oh yeah," I said, remembering that Twila had mentioned it. I hadn't even noticed if it was open when I left. "Do you know who closed it? It wasn't open when my dad and I came back."

"Someone was assigned that job. Maybe Daria?" She shook out one arm. "What does that matter anyway?"

"I'm just trying to figure out what could have happened."

"The police will do that," she said, sounding like she was about to dismiss me.

As much as I wanted to stop running, I had a job to do. "Do you know anything about Twila outside of our group?"

"Like what?" she asked.

"I don't know," I said. "Did she like Pinterest? Or online poker? Or collecting something weird, like Star Trek toys?"

She didn't smile at my joke. "She never talked about anything like that," she said. "Just family stuff and her puzzle business."

I felt a stitch in my side from trying to keep up with her. I better get to the point so I could stop running before I collapsed. "One of the other moms thought Twila was mad at one of the SPM members." I took a deep breath. "Do you know anything about that?"

Gina came to a sliding halt, and I took a couple of steps past her before stopping. Even her reflexes were faster than mine.

"Are you questioning me?" Her voice was too loud for the park. Several adults turned to stare at us and Baby Joyce stopped making cute noises and looked up at her warily. Gina moved closer to me and spoke in a quieter tone that still sounded angry. "Are you trying to get the police to suspect someone other than you?"

"No!" I said.

Baby Joyce whimpered.

I changed to a sing-song happy tone. "I'm just following up on something one of the other moms said."

"Who?"

No way was I throwing Daria under the bus. "I'm not sure."

She stared at me and I decided I better come clean. Besides, I needed someone in the group on my side or this investigation was going to be over before it really began.

"Okay," I said. "*I* know I didn't kill Twila. Whoever did it is trying to frame me. I just want to make sure the police look into every possibility, because you know what? I have to clear my name. And you know what else?" My voice started to get louder. "Whoever did that to Twila could do it again. I have to do what I can to make sure that doesn't happen to anyone else."

By the end of my little speech, I'd totally forgotten little Joyce and was practically yelling. She blinked up at me and wailed.

Gina didn't even look mad. She simply picked up Joyce, put her on her shoulder, and started swaying with a thoughtful look on her face. Then she started mini-squats as if they were automatic. Joyce stuck her thumb in her mouth and calmed down right away.

"Look," Gina said, not breathing hard at all. "None of us had any reason to hurt Twila. We're all just trying to make a little extra money for our families. Nothing worth killing someone over."

I made my voice quiet. "Money's not the only motive for murder."

"Passion?" She paused, thinking it through. "You think she was fooling around on her husband or something?"

I shrugged awkwardly. "As I said, I didn't know her very well."

She shook her head emphatically. "That's Mona's department," she said. "Not Twila's. She worked too hard to get her family and loved them too much to risk anything that would hurt them."

Mona's department? "Worked too hard?" I asked.

"Twila was very open about being adopted as a young child. When she couldn't have children, she adopted her two boys," Gina said. "Those kids were everything to her."

"Do you know her husband?" I asked.

"Trent? Not very well," she said. "He's some kind of consultant and travels a lot."

"I don't want to be a gossip, but one of our members mentioned that Twila thought one of us was doing something unethical. You know everyone a lot more than I do. Could you, I don't know, ask around a little?"

"You mean, help you clear your name and implicate someone else." Her voice was flat, but at least she didn't seem angry anymore.

"Only if that person is the real killer," I said.

She thought for a minute, and then nodded. "I'll do what I can."

It felt good to have one person on my side, even if she was only helping reluctantly.

Then she looked me up and down. "You should join one of my classes. We'll get rid of that paunch in no time."

Paunch?

Chapter 9

Saturdays were all about getting ready for the Little Italy Farmers' Market. I was so used to waking up early that I opened my eyes before dawn again. Then I remembered that today was the day. Twila's funeral.

Even if I didn't have the farmers' market, there was no way I could go to the funeral. If any of Twila's family members or friends believed I had something to do with her death, I couldn't even imagine what seeing me would do to them.

I had drafted an email to the SPM group but never sent it. I hoped they understood why I couldn't be there. Lani said she was going in my place, which made me feel marginally better. She'd also given herself the task of seeing if anyone was acting suspicious.

While I was getting dressed, Trouble brought me a puzzle piece covered with dust. What the heck? Where did she find this? She sat staring up at me. What was she trying to tell me? It was almost like she understood how sad it made me to not be able to pay my respects. Or was she trying to tell me something else?

"Thank you?" I said, which seemed to satisfy her.

I really had to get out more.

* * * *

Setting up in the familiar chaos of the farmers' market gave me something to focus on besides the funeral. Trouble sat contentedly in her carrier until I had the tables covered and all my products arranged in attractive piles. I set up her cat chair—a tiny little loveseat that Elliott had found on Amazon. It was the same shade of blue as my labels. Trouble graciously allowed me to put her on her perch, but I waited until customers began appearing before putting on her hat. As long as she got enough attention from her fans, she usually didn't complain about the tiny elastic band that held it in place on her cute little head.

She sniffed a little as if to say *I'm doing this for you, but I don't like it,* and tilted her head at the first group that came by.

"Is that a real cat?" one woman said, before heading over to pet her.

I swear Trouble smirked at me.

Gypsy Sue waved hello on her way to her booth in the next section. The Little Italy Farmers' Market was spread out over several blocks. Sue stopped by after she was done setting up and before the crowds grew. "Hey, did you get that other nonsense taken care of?"

"What do you mean?" I asked.

"Finding out who killed your friend?" she said.

I wasn't sure how to answer. "You think I'm looking into that?"

She gave me a sardonic look. "How long have I known you?"

"Wait," I said. "Are you really psychic? I've never been able to figure it out."

"Psychic enough to know you're not answering me." She went back to her booth.

Luckily, the market was too busy to allow me to dwell on my problems, although it was harder to be "on" today, especially remaining friendly to one woman who decided to challenge me about why "human grade" ingredients were important for cats.

People who came to my booth were usually interested in finding out how to help their cats get healthier, not denying the whole need for healthier food. My potential customers were often very educated about what their cats needed. They'd done a lot of research and were hesitant to try something new once they found products that worked. But then I could point to all the research I'd done, and give them information on my formulas. And a free sample went a long way too.

"Some animals have health issues that are aggravated by the ingredients in bulk food," I explained, with a lot less patience than I normally had.

"My cat eats what's on sale," she said. "You're just trying to take advantage of all of the idiots who treat their pets like kids."

Trouble turned to her and narrowed her eyes.

Uh-oh.

"You're so lucky to have such a healthy cat," I tried, turning on the charm.

But she was on a roll. "And I heard that all that organic crap was just nonsense."

"That's not what our research has found," I said. "Why don't you take a free sample and see if your cat likes it." I handed her a can of Chicken Sauté. "Let me know next week how it goes."

Then I turned my back on her to talk to a potential customer who had been watching the exchange. "Can I help you?"

"Yes," she said. "I'd like to buy some of your organic food for my cat who I spoil mercilessly."

I looked over my shoulder to make sure Disagreeable Lady was on her way. "You're at the right place, apparently."

"You handled that well," she said.

"Thanks," I said. "All in a day's work."

She bought half a box of my cans, probably more than she intended, to make up for the unpleasant woman.

During a lull in customer traffic, I checked my phone and saw a text from Lani. *Want to meet at Pico's for an early dinner?*

I was dying to call her and find out everything I could about the funeral, but face to face would be better. I packed up when the flow of customers had slowed, and stopped at home to drop everything off.

I walked in while my dad was giving another lesson to Elliott.

"Mom! Listen to my G chord." He strummed the guitar. "I'm learning 'On Top of Old Smokey.'"

As soon as I set the cat carrier down, Trouble strolled out and headed to the kitchen. Probably for a bowl check and to get a snack. Or maybe to escape the excruciatingly slow rendition of Elliott's song.

My dad's eyes carefully watched Elliott's fingers and he looked up at the end of the song. "He's really good at reading music," he said with a proud smile.

"It's all that singing," I said. "Great job, kiddo."

Elliott grinned and put the guitar carefully against the wall.

"I'm meeting Lani for dinner at Pico's," I told them. "What do you guys want me to bring back?"

"Cool!" Elliott said. "Beef burrito grande."

"Chicken chimichangas," my dad said, reaching out for his wallet on the side table. "Here, let me give you some money."

"Dad," I said firmly. "I got it. The farmers' market was great today."

He grumbled a little, but I was pleased that he was hungry enough to order a big meal.

Since I'd moved to Sunnyside, Lani and I had become regulars at Pico's, a hole-in-the-wall Mexican restaurant on the outskirts of the small downtown area. Pico Sanchez had bought an out-of-business diner and didn't bother to change the décor. He'd simply plastered a Pico's sign over the Sunnyside Diner sign.

Sunnyside didn't get a lot of tourists, but plenty of people on their way to and from San Diego stopped at Pico's, expecting burgers and fries. They all left happy with the best tacos, burritos, and quesadillas in Southern California, which was saying a lot. College kids came all the way out from San Diego, and Pico even got his fair share of young professionals who liked the odd setting for Mexican food.

Pico was the size of a small giant, always wearing a sauce-spattered apron that he must buy in bulk from the Hagrid clothing line at the department store. The first time Lani had introduced me as her best friend, he'd wrapped me in a huge, gentle hug that he repeated every time we came.

I'd quickly learned that he was as harmless as they come and as gossipy as a mother hen.

"How you doin' girl?" he asked as he passed by me, delivering chips and spicy salsa to a table full of men in golf shirts while his son delivered tangy frozen margaritas.

"Good," I said, a moment before one of his famous hugs.

He looked down at me as if trying to figure out how I was feeling. "Lani told me the news. What are those Keystone Cops thinking?"

I laughed. "Well, one of them seems to know what she's doing."

"That lady detective?" he asked. "Yeah, she's good."

"You know her?" I asked.

"I know everybody, girl," he said. "Or at least someone who knows everyone."

Pico's burritos were legendary, filled to the brim with delicious beef, pulled pork, or chicken. Just thinking about them made my mouth water, especially added to the scent of simmering sauce, sautéing onions and peppers, and that bite of hot pepper in the air.

Lani was sitting in a booth against the wall, a sure sign that she wanted to talk away from Pico and his sons. She had a margarita waiting for me and was already scooping up the spicy salsa with chips. Today she was wearing a white silky top with unicorns painted on the fabric.

"Hope that's not what you wore to the funeral," I said.

"Funny," she answered through chip. "I do own one normal black dress."

"I can't imagine that," I said. "Did Piper make you buy it?"

She smiled. "Of course. For just such occasions."

Pico came by to take our order and Lani asked him, "What's the latest you've heard?"

"Not much yet," he said. "For what it's worth, we got cops here a lot and none of them think you done it."

"Really?" I asked, surprised and happy that my innocence was being talked about so openly. Or maybe Pico was just good at eavesdropping.

"Well, all 'cept that Little guy," Pico said. "He's like a dog with a bone. Just don't let go."

"What are other people, the ones who aren't police, saying?" Lani asked.

He shrugged. "Some of 'em think you hurt that girl, but I always tell 'em off," he said. "Everyone loves your dad and I told 'em to shut their pie hole. No daughter of Hank's would do something so terrible."

"Aw, thank you Pico," I said. *I think.*

He nodded for emphasis and walked back to the kitchen.

I dropped a bunch of chips on my plate and squeezed lime on them, and then sprinkled salt on top. "Okay," I said. "Tell me everything."

Lani filled me in on the funeral, which was heartbreaking. Twila's two boys, ages eight and ten, had seemed all cried out. They were stoic, until the very end of the funeral, when they both broke down and had to be taken into another room by an aunt.

Twila's husband, Trent, was tall and handsome. "He should totally be put on the list," she said.

"Because he's handsome?" I asked.

"Yes," she said. "Maybe he was having an affair."

"Did you ever meet Twila?" I asked. "She was adorable. And smart. And nice."

"Just put him on the list," she insisted.

"Were the police there?" I asked.

"I didn't see anyone who looked like police," Lani said. "But there were a lot of people. Maybe I didn't notice them."

She had recognized some of the SPM members from the photos I'd shown her and lurked around them as long as she could without anyone noticing. She hadn't heard anything worthwhile, except one of them wondering why I wasn't there. "She made it seem all suspicious," Lani said.

I couldn't help but feel hurt. "Which one was it?"

"I'm not sure," she said. "I heard it but couldn't tell whose voice it was."

"Why would anyone say something like that?" Maybe I should have sent that email. I filled her in on my conversation with Gina.

"Two down—Gina and Daria," she said. "Who are you going after next?"

"The others are hard," I said. "But I have a plan for Fawn."

"Do you want me to talk to her?" Lani asked. "I have a board meeting for that foster youth nonprofit with her next week."

"Was she at the funeral?" I asked.

"Yep," she said. "We said hi, but she left right after the service."

"I could make an appointment with her as a life coach," I said. "So it won't be so obvious."

"That's a way better idea than me trying to grab her after the meeting," Lani said. "You can figure out some stuff while you ask her questions."

Wait. "What stuff?"

"Um," she said. "You know. Life goals and stuff. I heard she's good at making you write them down and figure out how to achieve them."

That made me pause. Thinking about my goals made me very uncomfortable. Like if I made plans, that meant I automatically jinxed them, and they'd never happen. "She also handles our group website and a bunch of the members' sites."

"Ooh," she said. "Good thought. Maybe she can see if one of the moms was up to something."

"She's not going to hack anyone, for heaven's sake," I said. "But maybe she knows stuff."

"What about the rest of your list?"

The other members were harder. "What reason could I use to talk to Mona? Or Bronx?" Then I had an idea. "Wait. Doesn't your mother-in-law have dogs? Do you think she'd let me borrow one for a grooming?"

"That's a great idea," she said. "Let me text her."

Her mother-in-law texted right back that anytime Sunday afternoon worked.

"Tomorrow?" I asked.

"May as well get it done," Lani said.

I brought up Bronx's website. "I can schedule it right here." I put in Sunday's date and three openings popped up. "How about one in the afternoon?"

She texted again. "That works for her," she said. "And she'll pay you back for the grooming."

I finished filling out the information just as Pico delivered Lani's quesadilla and my chicken enchiladas. Both were piled high with melted cheese, guacamole, and sour cream. We dove in.

My phone lit up and I picked it up, expecting a confirmation email from Bronx. It was an email from Twomey's Health Food.

I felt cold. And then hot. And then cold again. "Oh man."

"What is it?" Lani asked. She jumped up and slid into my side of the booth while I clicked on the email and waited as the little widget spun for what felt like an eternity. Then the email appeared.

Dear Ms. Summers,

My heart started pounding.

We appreciate your interest in becoming a supplier for Twomey's Health Food. You have been selected—

Oh. My. God.

...to be one of several local organic pet food suppliers asked to submit business proposals outlining how your company would be able to work with Twomey's.

Please submit your proposal by 5:00 pm on Friday, June 16.

A week?

We will let you know our decision on which, if any, of the selected businesses were chosen in approximately two weeks.

Thank you for your interest in joining the Twomey's family.

"Wow," I said at the same time Lani squealed.

"That's so exciting!" She hugged my arm.

"Yeah, it is," I said, my mind spinning.

"How's that proposal going?" she asked. "You started on it, right?"

I nodded, wondering if my efforts were too amateurish for a real company like Twomey's.

"Okay," she said, moving back to her own side of the table. "I know you like to be a lone wolf and all, but hear me out. I have a business advisor who is a genius at all of this. I think you should meet with him."

"I can't afford—"

"He's a volunteer with SCORE, you know, that organization of retired executives who help out new businesses?" she explained. "I'm telling you, he could help."

"What do I need him for?" I asked.

"He's a freaking genius," she said. "Just talk to him. He's like a combination of one of those Shark Tank guys and Oprah."

"What does that even mean?" I asked.

"Like really smart *and* nice and encouraging. If you're lucky," she continued, "he'll take a real interest in you and become your unofficial business advisor like he is with me."

I bristled. "I don't need that."

"Actually, you don't know what you need to take it to the next level." She paused as if choosing her words carefully. "He'll help you in ways you can't imagine right now."

I must have been feeling particularly unsure of myself because suddenly I was agreeing and she was typing an introductory email on her phone. "He's brilliant, really. And he'll love you—he has a soft spot for single moms because of his own mother."

She looked up, worried that she'd offended me. "But that's not why he'll help you. He really likes entrepreneurs. He was very poor as a kid and created a bunch of businesses. He's rich now, like really rich. He wants to help people who have overcome difficulty as he did."

"What businesses?" I asked.

"You know Powell Theaters? That's one. East Village Bowling Alleys. He named it that because he grew up in the east part of San Diego. And he has Come and Get It Restaurants."

"Wow," I said. "Those are all over California."

"Yep," she said. "He's a master at franchising. And he's also a venture capitalist. If he decides to invest in you, you'll have it made."

I went silent. Lani seemed to read my mind.

"I didn't introduce you to him before because I thought you'd say no. You were determined to do it all on your own. You're stubborn, you know. But you're going to need him now. With this Twomey's deal, you're going big time."

* * * *

Big time.

Lani's words rang in my ears as I pulled up my fledgling proposal. That was easy for her to say.

Still, I couldn't stop thinking about it. What did "big time" mean to me?

I checked my phone for the zillionth time. I didn't know why I kept checking. It was eight on a Saturday night. Surely, businessman Quincy had better things to do.

Then I saw it. A response from Mr. Powell. Maybe he didn't have better things to do.

Dear Colbie, bff of Lani, ☺

I would love to learn more about your business and how I may help. Would you like to meet at the El Cajon Rental Kitchen Tuesday morning?

Tuesday? Could I finish a draft of the proposal by then? I thought about my schedule. I could do it.

I emailed him back that it worked for me, and asked for the time and address, feeling like I was taking a step into the unknown.

Chapter 10

There's no such thing as a day off for a small business owner, but Sundays usually included some amount of down time. I always made a big breakfast for Elliott, and now my dad, and tried to do something fun. Of course, I still had to fit in some of the background stuff, like catching up on accounting and getting as much of the social media marketing out of the way as I could. I scheduled the upcoming week's outgoing messages ahead of time so I didn't have to think about them.

And today I had the added fun of working on my proposal and questioning Bronx while she groomed my dog-for-a-day.

In honor of Elliott's musical, this morning's special was pancakes in the shape of *The Cat in the Hat*, with cherry juice dribbled over whipped cream to decorate the red bow and make the lines in the hat, and chocolate sauce for the body.

"Elliott!" I called upstairs. "Breakfast."

I opened the back door to let my dad know it was ready and took a moment to appreciate the view. The marine layer was moving back to the west and the sun was peeking through, throwing shafts of light onto the cornfield in the distance. "It's beautiful out here."

He patted the chair beside him. "Come have a sit."

"Maybe later," I said. "Breakfast is ready and the whipped cream will soon be 'soupy cream.'"

He needed both armrests to push himself to his feet, making me worry yet again. He'd always seemed so big and strong to me. How could one illness do this to him?

I watched him take a seat at the table before walking over to the stairs again. "Elliott," I called up, my mom voice clearly saying, *"Now."*

"Sorry," he said, yawning as he came down the stairs, slowly for once. "I was up late learning lines." Then he saw the pancakes. "Cat in the Hat? Cool!"

"Sit down so we can eat," my dad said with pretend grumpiness, and we all dug in.

"I'm going to visit the chicks, later," Elliott said, with food in his mouth. I raised my eyebrows and he swallowed before adding, "Sorry."

That gave me the opportunity to ask the burning question. "I didn't know Joss had a daughter." I tried to sound nonchalant.

"Yeah," Elliott said while he started mixing the cherry-flavored cream with the chocolate. "This is like a banana split. For breakfast!"

I brought him back to the topic at hand. "How old is she?"

He shrugged. "Never met her."

My dad answered. "She's ten. Her name's Kai. It's Hawaiian or something. He's divorced. That's why he moved here from Alaska to be closer to her."

"He's from Alaska?" It sounded so exotic. But I guess people from Alaska thought Southern California was exotic.

"Yep," Elliott said. "He's got a bunch of art from there. And a moose head named Joe!"

"Joe?" I asked. "He brought a moose head all the way from Alaska?"

"It's special to his daughter," my dad said, sounding a little defensive.

Elliott changed the subject, sounding both excited and anxious. "My old group never did a whole musical at camp. Just pieces of them."

"I'm sure your director knows what he's doing," I said. "He's been working with youth theater for years."

"I know," he said. "I just have a lot of lines to learn."

"You'll be great," I said.

"When are you picking up that dog?" Elliott asked.

"A little before one," I said.

"I wish we had a dog," he said.

Trouble had been walking through the kitchen and stopped dead in her tracks. She looked over her shoulder like she totally understood him, and gave a loud, "Meow."

We all understood what that meant. *When hell freezes over, buddy.*

"I couldn't agree more. We've got enough Trouble already," my dad said.

* * * *

I went up to let Elliott know I was heading out to get the dog early so the little guy could get used to this place before Bronx got here for his grooming.

"Hey, Mom?" He scooted back to sit against the headboard and then started to say something but stopped.

I sat down on the bed. "What's up, kiddo?"

"Do you think...my dad might want to meet me?" His voice started off tentative and ended in a whisper.

My stomach clenched. Oh man. I knew this moment had to come, but now was just about the worst possible time.

"I know he didn't want me. But maybe..." He took a deep breath. "Maybe he'd want to hear how I'm doing now, or something."

I'd thought about how I'd handle this so many times, but all of my plans flew out of my head. "He might," I said, wondering if I was telling him the truth.

He kept talking. "You said that some people aren't meant to be parents. But, like, Joss is trying really hard to get custody of his daughter."

"That's true," I said.

"My...dad is really old now. Like thirty-three." His voice was earnest. "Maybe he's, I don't know, matured."

I took a deep breath and asked, "What would you like to do?" I was proud of how calm I kept my voice in spite of the anxiety crawling up my spine.

"I don't know. Maybe friend him on Facebook or something?"

I paused. "Do you want me to contact him first?"

He shook his head. "I'll do it. I know his name," he admitted. "You had it in the browser once and I looked him up."

"Okay," I said. "I knew you'd want to meet him, when you were ready."

"He's like a manager now," Elliott said. "And I, I look just like him."

I nodded. "Okay," I repeated. My hands started to shake and I put them under my legs. "Should we contact him now?" My voice was a little too high, but Elliott didn't seem to notice.

"Yeah," he said. "Now would be good."

* * * *

I got through it, somehow remaining upbeat even though I believed that it would only lead to heartache. I kept up the smile until I left Elliott alone in his room, heading downstairs and past the living room door with a strangled, "I gotta go."

Trouble jumped off my dad's lap with a loud meow but I kept going. Out the front door to the street where I started walking and blubbering like a baby.

Why was I having this reaction?

Elliott was getting to an age where he could use a man's perspective. Even though I made sure we had adult guy friends that he could count on and that he had a relationship with my dad, I knew he'd want to meet his biological father someday. It was perfectly normal.

How had I ever gotten messed up with Richard Winston the Third? We'd met when we were students at the University of California San Diego. He was the first in his family to not make it into Yale. He once confessed that he did it on purpose so he could escape his family's plans for him. And to surf every day that he could.

I was in my own surfing phase and fell head over heels. I found out I was pregnant on Halloween. It was a total shock. We both committed to telling our parents over Thanksgiving. I told my dad, who had a complete meltdown, and that's when I moved out. I was in such a white-hot rage at his reaction, that I'm not sure if he kicked me out or if I told him I was leaving.

Richard never came back. He sent me a letter saying to never contact him again and included a large check from his father. According to friends we had in common, his father wrote a much larger check to Yale and Richard transferred there. I dropped out of school and lost touch with those friends, but couldn't help but Google him once in a while. He'd gone on to get an MBA and work in his father's financial services company.

Maybe he'd finally matured enough to want to meet his son. I hoped Elliott hadn't created a fairy tale where he and his dad would develop a wonderful relationship and live happily ever after.

I didn't even notice which way I was walking until I tripped on the sidewalk in front of Horace's house and fell hard on my knees.

"Whoa there, girl," he said. Moving faster than anyone his age should be able to, he helped me up. "You okay?"

The concern in his voice was so different from the first time I'd met him. "I'm fine." I brushed off his arm, but then I winced. My knees were a mess.

"Come up to the porch where it's cool," Horace said. "You gotta clean up those scrapes."

"I can do it at home," I insisted.

"You don't wanna show your boy or your dad those knees," he said. "Or those tears, I expect."

Somehow I was walking along beside him, although I was careful not to put any weight on his arm. He had seemed so much larger on his porch, when he barely came to my shoulder, with a thin build made gaunt by age.

"Sit, sit," he said. "I'll be right out."

I followed his orders, and sat in a wooden rocking chair that was solid and comfortable. The shock of hitting the ground so hard had stopped my crying. I was down to intermittent sniffles and feeling sorry for myself.

He came out holding a small first aid kit in one hand and a tall glass of iced tea with the other. "I hope it's okay it's sweetened."

I took it from him, grateful. "That's perfect."

"I hope you don't drink that chemical sugar crap," Horace said. "It'll turn your insides black." He waited for me to take a sip and set the glass down on the small table in between the chairs before giving me a wet paper towel and a first aid kit. "You want to do this yourself?"

I nodded, taking it from him. My right knee had caught the worst of it and I focused on getting the dirt out of it.

"Your kid make you upset like that?" He looked off into distance, which made it easier for me to answer.

"He wants to find his dad," I said with a hitch in my voice.

"Ah," he said. "I know you probably don't want to listen to an ol' coot like me, but I'm gonna give you my advice anyways."

"Okay," I said, dabbing on some antibiotic cream.

"I assume his dad was a jerk back when he was a boy." He said it like he already knew.

I nodded. "A big one."

"Here's what I know," he said. "He's still gonna be a jerk. You go ahead and let your boy talk to him. Your little man is smart. He'll figure it out right quick."

"But what if...?" I couldn't even put into words what I was worried about.

"You tell him not to do it, he'll end up still doing it and be mad at you about it," he said. "Your boy loves you. No one is going take that away. You just gotta let him."

I sniffed, and started working on the other knee.

"Now you finish bandaging yourself up and get on home before he figures out you're upset. You let it take its course, and you betcha you'll both be fine."

* * * *

Elliott hadn't even noticed I'd been gone. I changed quickly and headed out. My idea to question Bronx by borrowing a dog and getting it groomed was more subtle than my first approaches. I was feeling a little proud of myself when I knocked on the door of Lani's mother-in-law's house. That is, until I heard the ferocious barking of at least two dogs.

I took a couple of steps back, as if they might come crashing through the wood, like the pitcher in a Kool-Aid commercial.

The door opened and a tiny older woman peeked out. "You must be Colbie," Mrs. Osmond said, pushing two snarling English bulldogs back with what must be her incredibly strong leg. "This is Hulk—he has the lightning mark on his forehead, just like Harry Potter, right? But we went with the Avengers for their names. And this little guy with the bum leg is Thor. Hold on for a minute while I get their leashes." She closed the door, probably to save my life.

Hulk? Thor? Wait, leashes? As in more than one?

She was soon back with both dogs, who had stopped growling and were now happily scrambling to get outside. They dashed through the door right past me to pee on the strip of green that lined the walkway, staring at me with slobbering, breathing-through-their-nose delight.

She handed me both leashes. What was going on?

"These things are a little tricky," she said. "Click that red button to shorten the leash."

"But," I tried, feeling overwhelmed.

"Thank you so much for taking them today," she said. "I know you'll have a blast. They growl a bit but don't ever bite. They are really the sweetest creatures." She bent down and grabbed the face of one (Thor?) while the other took off toward the road, the leash making a zinging sound as it let out. "You be good for Aunt Colbie."

Aunt Colbie? I frantically pushed the red button, but it didn't help. The dog didn't stop until the leash hit the end, at least fifteen feet away, and he came to a stop, jerking my arm nearly out of its socket and taking a comical tumble, his back legs flying up and around until he was facing me, looking surprised.

"He's fine," she said. "He does that all the time." Then she handed me a bag of dishes and toys. Wait. How long did she think I'd have them?

She escaped inside with such a relieved expression that I knew I'd been conned. Lani had called her a kind and gentle steamroller and now I knew what she meant.

Both dogs decided to explore different sides of the yard and to keep myself from being toppled over like a scene from a Three Stooges movie, I put a foot on each of the leashes and yelled, "Stop! Heel!"

Of course, they didn't listen. They were having too good of a time. But I could slowly reel them in a little closer with each of their dashes across the grass, and jam on the leash lock. In a few minutes, they were sitting at my feet, their tongues hanging out and looking very pleased with themselves, while I was breathless and sweaty.

I noticed the drool coming from both of them. It was a good thing my car was old. "Okay, Hulk and Thor. Want to go for a drive?"

I swear they grinned at the word "drive" and in a split second they were up and running toward the car, towing me along like a reluctant toddler. "Slow down!"

They turned their heads toward each other, their scrunched-in faces seeming to laugh at me together. They continued to tug me along, surprisingly strong for their size. I opened the back door and they jumped in with effort, their squat bodies squirming and scrambling to get up on the seat.

Hulk immediately went to the opposite window and squished his face against it. I reached down to help Thor, trying to give him a hand so his leg had something to push up on. But then he slid and I ended up scooting him up by his butt. Ugh. I closed the door. How did little Ms. Osmond handle them? She was either stronger than she appeared, or they behaved better with her.

By the time I made it around the car to my own door, Hulk had jumped into my seat and had his face smashed up against my window, leaving behind a huge smear of dog snot. I pushed him over to the passenger seat with difficulty, especially since Thor decided he wanted to sit there too. They pushed shoulders against each other as if fighting over the front. I guess dogs couldn't call, "Shotgun!"

The smell of dog breath whooshed by me. I hoped the grooming included brushing their teeth and administering some super-powered mouthwash. But their enthusiasm was kind of charming. "Okay, boys," I said. "Let's do this."

I blasted the air conditioning, and as soon as the air turned cold, they shoved their noses toward the vents. The trip home was uneventful, other than driving carefully so they wouldn't slide off the front seat into the dashboard. I learned that lesson after stopping for the first stop light.

I pulled into the driveway with a heavy sigh and put their leashes on just as Bronx arrived, efficiently angling her little trailer to back into our driveway. She hopped out of her car and waved. "Hey, Colbie." She looked confused when she saw the dogs tumbling out of my car. "That's Thor and Hulk. I thought I was washing y'all's dog."

Great. I'd chosen two dogs who were already her clients. What were the odds of that?

They dragged me along, running right up to her and wriggling with delight as she rubbed her hands on their backs. "Hello, my good boys," she said in that tone people use for puppies and babies.

"Uh, no." I put on my confused face as if I had no idea how she got that idea. "I'm watching my friend's mother's dogs and thought it would be a nice treat for them. And her."

"Cool!" she said, happy with the double customer bonus. "Let me set up." She opened the trailer door and put down the ramp, then climbed inside.

Hulk sat at the bottom of the ramp, panting and waiting impatiently.

She looked outside and laughed. "Y'all like to be first, right Hulk?"

Thor sniffed around the wheels before taking his seat with Hulk.

"Can I see inside?"

"Sure." She grabbed a hose coming from the ceiling to a couple of hooks, aimed it into the tub, and turned the water on. "Water tank on the roof," she explained. Then she raised a pneumatic table in the center of the trailer. Hulk growled as Thor put a paw on the ramp and then backed off, as if knowing it wasn't his turn.

"This is great," I said. "You have everything you need."

Bronx flipped a few switches and tested the temperature of the water against her wrist. Then she sneezed loudly.

"Bless you," I said, taking a step back and wondering if I should be in an enclosed place with her.

She sneezed again. Six more times. I stopped saying, "Bless you," after the third and waited until she seemed to be finished. "Are you okay?" I asked.

"Oh, yes," she said. "I'm allergic to dogs." She pulled out an inhaler, breathed out as if getting every bit of air out, and then took a puff of her medication.

"You are?" I asked.

She nodded, holding her breath for a long time and then exhaling. "Sorry. But I love them so much. I just suck down the meds and I'm fine." She took Hulk's leash. "Let's get this party started."

"Is it okay if I watch?" I asked.

"Sure," she said.

I stepped up into the trailer with Thor on my heels. "How long have you had this business?"

She opened a small door cut into the side of the tub and Hulk jumped right in. "About two years."

"Is it better than having a store?" I watched her spray water all over Hulk, rubbing his fur as if to smush the water in more. He closed his eyes, enjoying the massage.

"Oh yeah." She poured a small amount of shampoo onto her hands and started lathering him up. A citrus scent mixed with wet dog smell. "It's much more affordable than rent, once you pay off the trailer and all this stuff. And I get to set my own hours."

I turned to check out her assortment of shampoos and conditioners. "How did you hear about Sunnyside Power Moms?"

"I'm not sure," she said. "Maybe when I was taking Gina's class."

I turned back. "Mommy and Me?"

She nodded, checking around Hulk's ears.

"Did you know Twila well?" I asked. "I'm still so upset about...everything."

"I can imagine." She sounded sympathetic. "I only saw her at meetings."

"Do you remember what happened that night?" I asked, and then backtracked when I realized how obvious it sounded. "I mean, I know the police talked to everyone. I just can't stop wondering."

Bronx looked up at me, pausing in her work, and Hulk decided to shake. Soapy dog water sprayed everywhere. She laughed, and the tense moment was gone. "I left with the last group—Daria, Sharon, Fawn, and Gina—and Twila was still there. She said she was almost done packing up her stuff, and yours, I guess. And then she was going to do a walk through and lock up." She pulled out the hose to rinse off the suds.

Oh man. Twila stayed later because of my stuff? I'd never even considered that. "That's all, huh?" My throat got so tight that my voice squeaked. "Nothing interesting happened during the trade show?"

She shook her head and then frowned, her forehead puckering. "You know, right before we left, she got a phone call that seemed to upset her."

"How could you tell?" I asked.

"She was all friendly, and then she answered the phone, and then she wasn't," she said.

Whoa. That was new information. "Did anyone ask her about it?"

She crinkled her forehead again, trying to remember. "No. At least, I don't think so. We were all carrying a bunch of stuff, and trying to hold the door for each other. It was a little confusing."

I remembered the business cards that had been left on her table. "Hey, did you ever figure out who the Lice Club Lady was?"

She laughed. "Ooh. I asked around, and it's some big secret."

"What do you mean?"

"Well, it makes sense. Some moms don't want anyone to know their kid has lice, so they have a secret place to go to get rid of them." She pulled out the blow dryer with a big diffuser attached to it. "They pay for the service, and no one's the wiser."

Thor decided he was bored with our conversation. He barked and put his paws on the side of the tub.

"It's almost your turn, honey," Bronx said. "Hey, can you take him for a walk while I dry Hulk? Sometimes that big guy decides he needs to go in the tub. That's a mess you don't want to see."

* * * *

A short time later, I called Ms. Osmond to take her clean and happy dogs back with their snazzy green bandanas wrapped around their necks, but she didn't answer.

Uh-oh.

I tried Lani, who laughed and said she'd track her mother-in-law down, and then I called Elliott and asked him to bring out a big bowl of water.

"Cool!" He knelt down to pet the dogs, and they took turns drinking the water and lapping his face with drooly slurps.

I couldn't help but cringe, but he loved it. "Can I take them for a walk?"

"Be my guest," I said.

Lani called back. "The good news is that I found my mother-in-law."

"And the bad news?"

"She's in Nordstrom Rack."

"Okay," I said. "When will she be home?"

"It's the Rack. It could be days."

Chapter 11

It was way too hot to leave the dogs outside. The only solution was to lock Trouble up in the bathroom and let the dogs into the house. Elliott kept them outside while I took my life into my own hands.

Trouble must have known what I was planning, because she dashed under my dad's bed as soon as I came into the house. Her snarl sounded like, *"You'll never catch me alive, coppers!"*

I could've simply closed the bedroom door, but since she might be vindictive enough to express her displeasure in another way—she'd once objected to me being late with her breakfast by peeing on my pillow—I was forced to lie down on the floor and pull her out by two legs. She calmed down as soon as I had her in my arms, simply glaring at me and probably plotting her revenge while I locked her in the downstairs bathroom where she couldn't do much damage.

The dogs were delighted to be inside, dashing around and exploring, shoving their noses into my dad's lap and then taking off to snuffle enthusiastically at the bathroom door before running up and down the stairs. Finally they plopped down onto the living room floor and Elliott petted them until they fell asleep.

We were definitely not getting a dog.

My dad started dozing off as well, so Elliott and I tiptoed out. He went back to learning lines and I texted Lani for a mother-in-law status. She sent back an emoji of a person shrugging.

I brought my laptop down to the kitchen and opened my proposal just as Lani called. Luckily I had the phone on vibrate and I answered with a whisper before heading into the laundry room and closing the door.

"I wanted to find out what Bronx said," she whispered back before realizing she wasn't the one who had to be quiet. "Why are we whispering?"

"My dad's sleeping, along with the dogs." I hopped up to sit on the washing machine and filled her in on what I'd learned.

"Damn," she said. "I wish we could find out more about that call Twila got. Maybe your police friend knows something."

"She's not my friend," I said. I debated telling her about Elliott wanting to contact his dad but decided to give the kid some privacy. I'd already told Horace all about it, and had to hope he'd be discreet. Instead, I told her what Bronx had said.

"Who's next on the list of suspects?" Then she said, "Hold on."

I heard some background noise and she yelled out playfully, "Your mother is taking advantage of my best friend."

"Oh no." Piper's voice came clearly through the phone. "What did she do now?"

Lani explained and Piper said, "I'll be right over to get them and take them home."

I was about to say it was okay when Trouble yowled from the bathroom, probably, *"Take the offer and get rid of those slobbering animals, you idiot!"*

"That would be great," I said to Lani.

"Piper's leaving for a medical convention later, but she has time now."

"That's really nice of her," I said. "I need to work on the proposal."

"Wait," Lani said. "Before we get to that, let's review the suspects. I have the document in front of me.

I smiled. "It's still funny to hear you say 'suspects' in your tough chick voice," I said.

"Yeah? What about 'perps'?"

I laughed. "Okay, what do you have written down?"

"Number one, Daria said Twila thought one of the SPM members was doing something unethical. Two, Gina doesn't know anything about that. She said that Twila was devoted to her family and wouldn't do anything to risk that, like have an affair. Three, Bronx said that Twila got a phone call that upset her, right before she and some of the other moms left together. You're making good progress."

"I'm not sure how to approach Mona," I said. "Or Sharon. My dad is pretty neat and doesn't need her closet organizing."

"For Mona, you could pretend that you're dating," she said. "Or that you're trying to get your hottie neighbor interested."

"Funny," I said. "I may have to stoop to that."

"Now tell me about the proposal."

I spent some time outlining my progress, until she interrupted me to say, "Piper's at your door but she doesn't want to wake your dad."

"On my way." I hung up and let Piper in. The dogs went crazy when they lifted their heads and saw who had arrived, totally defeating the no doorbell idea.

My dad blinked and sat up in his chair. "Hey, Piper."

"Nice to see you, Hank," she said. "Sorry to bother you. Just picking up the monsters."

"They were no trouble," he said. "Except to Trouble." He chuckled at his own joke.

"How's that cough?" she asked, as she expertly attached their leashes. I collected their dishes and toys for her.

"A little better," he said.

"Good," she said. "Don't hesitate to call if you want me to check it out." The dogs pulled her toward the door, and she called out over her shoulder, "Oh, my mom will send you a check for the grooming. If she has any money left after shopping!"

I started to rework my mission statement when a notification came up that another review had been posted to SDHelp. I clicked over.

G. Verde from Encinitas, California gave me a one star review! *Bought this at LI farmers market and my cat wouldn't eat it. Saw that the owner is a murder suspect! Wonder where she gets her meat?*

"What the hell?" I yelled.

"What's wrong?" my dad said.

I walked into the living room in disbelief. "Look!"

I handed him the laptop and he read it, his face turning into a determined scowl. "Hold on." He searched for *G. Verde Encinitas*, probably ready to track him down and give him a piece of his mind.

"It's okay, Dad," I said.

He waved me away. I sat on the armrest of his chair to see what he was up to. The search came back. There was no G. Verde in Encinitas, California.

I figured something out. "Verde is Green in Spanish. What is going on?"

"I don't know," he said. "But I have a guy who can find out."

* * * *

The next morning was Elliott's first day of musical theater camp. He'd jumped out of bed as soon as I opened his door to wake him up, both nervous and excited.

"Richard Winston the Third hasn't responded." He avoided looking at me by digging a spoon into his oatmeal.

"How do you feel about that?" I asked, channeling my best therapist rather than letting him know that this was exactly what I feared for him.

"I don't know," he said. "It was kind of bad timing, because I have to worry about this show. I wish…"

"What?"

"I should have put it off until everything was more, I don't know, figured out," he said.

I tried to reassure him. "Whatever happens, you'll be fine. *We'll* be fine."

After dropping him at the recreation center, I stopped at the grocery store to pick up dried cranberries. My cook had told me we were low and my normal supplier had a delay. I was searching for organic when I saw Sharon come down the aisle. I'd run into her at the same time last week. Damn. I'd been putting off talking to Sharon since I felt so bad for implicating her husband. And because she was so nice to everyone. And maybe because I was totally jealous of her organizational skills.

"Hi, Colbie," Sharon said.

"Same bat time. Same bat place," I joked. "We must be on the same grocery schedule."

"It's the least busy time here," Sharon said. "We missed you at the funeral."

My throat tightened even though she'd said it kindly. "I was so sorry that I couldn't be there."

"I know, sweetie." She patted my shoulder. "Grief is hard on all of us."

"How was it?" I asked.

She shook her head. "Beautiful. But…tragic. That poor family."

I took a deep breath. "It's just terrible."

"It is."

"Do you know them well? Her family, I mean." Was I really using a chance encounter at the grocery store to investigate a murder?

"No. We live in the next complex over, but her kids are much younger." She shook her head. "Her poor husband had to fly back from Paris."

So he couldn't have done it. I guess it isn't always the spouse. "I really hate to bother you with this, but you knew Twila a lot longer than I did. Someone mentioned that she was mad at one of the moms in our group. Did she say anything to you?"

"Mad?" She frowned and shook her head. "She never said anything like that. Why are you asking?"

I shrugged as if it wasn't a big deal. "It's been bothering me. I mean, she was so nice. And she did so much work organizing us. How could anyone be mad at her?"

Sharon moved her cart out of the way of a child pushing a kiddy shopping cart. "The only people who were mad at her were those people at the bottom of the list for Updale Estates."

I moved out of the way too. Those things were lethal on ankles. "What's that?"

"A new development that's supposed to be nice *and* affordable," she said. "Ever since the list was made public, people at the bottom have been accusing the people at the top of bribing the developers. And Twila and Trent were at the top."

"Wow," I said. "People will complain about anything." I couldn't imagine how that could have led to Twila's murder.

"It's more than that," she said. "There's some wacko activist getting people riled up and organizing protests—they even blocked the road so constructions crews couldn't get through. The affordable housing people are teaming up with the environmentalists and creating a big fuss."

My phone buzzed and I saw a text from Elliott. *So far, so good.* Then I noticed the time. Shoot. "Well, don't let me keep you. I have to get these cranberries to the kitchen."

"Thanks," she said. "I have a consult over in Santee."

Then I remembered the question I was supposed to ask all the SPM members. "Oh sorry. Someone called the Lice Club Lady left a bunch of cards on a table at the trade show. Do you know anything about her?"

Sharon scowled at me. "My children never had lice," she said, insulted.

"Of course not," I said. "Mine, neither. It was just a question..." Great. Now she'd really hate me.

I said good-bye and got out of there. It was refreshing to leave the small town, and the whole tragedy, behind and head toward San Diego. Maybe I was meant to be a city girl forever.

I noticed the traffic up ahead and got off at the next exit, winding my way to the kitchen through the streets.

My cook Zoey was already there, reading the day's batch sheets and pulling out ingredients. "'Morning," she said to me and then called out to the room, "I'll need Stove One in half an hour."

The commercial kitchen was too small for the four companies who shared it on Mondays and Tuesdays. Most of us wished we had enough business to justify our own kitchen, but we rented it only for the times we

could afford. We all worked hard to ensure the kitchen remained certified
and that we didn't interfere with each other's processes.

At the next table, someone yelled back over the high-pitched sound of
an industrial mixer. "Make sure you put on the fan. I don't want no fish
stink in my cupcakes."

"No problem," Zoey answered, although she rolled her eyes at me.

Zoey was a single mom and had gone through a similar program that
I had. Like me, she'd been given housing, daycare, training, a job, and
most important, a supportive community. Unfortunately, her ex-boyfriend
kept hanging around the restaurant where she worked, and they let her
go. With a restraining order in place, and no customers to contend with,
she could cook to her heart's delight in this kitchen. Once she had started
working for me two mornings a week, she'd been hired by a couple of
the other companies who used the same location, and now worked there
pretty much full time.

Today she used a tie-dyed scarf to cover her dyed-black hair—no
hairnets for her—and she wore a chef's coat over her clothes. She was
small and wiry, her thin arms somehow able to effortlessly carry three
boxes of Meowio food at a time.

"Shoot," Zoey said. "We're out of apple juice." She looked up at me,
hoping I'd drive to the closest store to pick it up.

I sighed, starting to take off the hairnet and gloves that I'd just put on.

"Take some of ours," one of the bakers said, handing it over. "It's organic."

"Thanks," Zoey said, but she read the label carefully to make sure
before setting it on the table. "I'm working on the sauté first. You want to
get on the seafood one? The vitamins are measured out over there." She
pointed with her chin to a small plastic bin filled with powder of various
shades of beige and yellow.

"Sure," I said, heading into the storage area to grab dried blueberries,
then into the refrigerator to pull out the fish and scallops, and then the
freezer to get the vegetables.

I dumped it all on the counter, careful to keep the raw ingredients
separate from what Zoey was working on. Then I pulled out the bin of
measuring cups and spoons, took a look at the batch sheet, and got to work.

"Hey," I said quietly to Zoey, the background noise of everyone's work
helping to keep our conversation private. I told her about the email from
Twomey's and the upcoming meeting with Lani's business consultant.
"Would you be able to work more hours for me if anything positive happens?"

"No prob," she said. "Just give me some lead time to sort out my schedule."

Oh good. One less thing to worry about.

* * * *

I'd made an afternoon appointment with Fawn, which she called a consultation. She wanted to make sure we were compatible as a life coach and coachee, or whatever she called her customers.

She'd directed me to avoid the front door and come to her office, which was a renovated garage. She lived in a neighborhood of McMansions that had at least two garages with most home owners using the second one for anything but a car garage, like for storage, workout room, or a man cave. I rang the doorbell beside a discreet copper plaque that said Fawn Escanso, Life Coach.

She answered right away, welcoming me into the beigest room I'd ever seen outside of a lawyer's office. Not that I'd been in a lot of those. It was all tasteful and felt very Zen, with a small fountain gurgling in the corner.

Fawn had big brown eyes with long lashes like a Disney princess. I suspected that she practiced keeping them wide open, or perhaps I was jealous since anytime I caught myself in the mirror, I had a thoughtful scowl on my face.

Normally, Fawn seemed business-like and no-nonsense, especially coming from her nonprofit meetings where she always wore a suit. Today she was dressed in what my dad would call "hippie" clothes. A flowy white shirt, lavender jeans, and sandals with flower decorations. Maybe her casual attire was supposed to help me to relax.

"Have a seat," she said, indicating the love seat that I assumed was her equivalent of a therapy couch. She sat in a wing back chair opposite me with an eager expression on her face.

"Thanks so much for fitting me in," I said, already feeling guilty that I wasn't really here for a consultation instead of questioning her about a murder.

"Of course," she said. "I love helping people, especially those I know."

I looked around. "You did a great job on this room."

"Thank you," she said. "Sharon helped me." She gestured toward the bookshelves behind her. Beige fabric bins had been placed artistically to provide pretty storage. "She organized my other business, and the big garage here too. Now we can get both cars in it."

"Very nice," I said. "So how does this work?"

"Today, I'm just going to ask you some questions that will most likely cause you to think about your life in different ways. You don't need to answer the questions, but I'll send them home with you as a sort of homework."

"Great," I said. "Just like my son."

She chuckled. "Well, a little different. Should we begin?"

I took a dramatic deep breath and smiled. "Yes."

"I'm going to read you five questions, and then you decide which of these you'd like to discuss today." She looked down and then met my eyes. "One. How happy are you today?"

Oh man. I looked away. That was a trick question. I was excited about my work possibilities, but my dad's illness and Twila's murder constantly lurked in the mind. And now I had the added worry of Elliott reaching out to his father.

She checked her notes and then met my eyes again, maintaining the same pleasant expression. "Two. What does success look like to you?"

Another hard one. I used to just want to make a living and support Elliott. Now, after Lani said I could go "big time," maybe I wanted more. But I wasn't sure exactly what that was.

"Three. What does success outside of work mean to you?"

Wait. Was she reading my mind?

I felt myself flush with a mixture of pride and embarrassment. Pride that I was raising a great kid. But that was about all I was doing outside of work. Although my relationship with my dad was getting better. I had some good friends. But I'd never had a successful romantic relationship. Like ever.

"Four. What negativity are you holding on to that keeps you from achieving success both inside and outside of your work?"

She really was reading my mind.

Fawn put her notebook down and folded her hands on top. "Which of those do you want to talk about?"

Which of those had the least chance of having to reveal anything private to her? "Um, success at work?"

"Excellent." She smiled. "Let's begin."

Chapter 12

Forty minutes later, I was a sweaty, much less coherent mess, and I still hadn't asked Fawn about Twila. "You really gave me a lot to think about." I stood up, trying not to look like I was running away. "My head is spinning. Can we stop here?"

"Of course." She moved to her desk and turned on her computer. "Let's meet next week so you can move your life forward. What days and times work best for you?"

Being a life coach must be a great excuse to nag. I pulled out my phone and brought up my calendar. "Next week is crazy," I said. "How about Friday afternoon the following week?"

I'd have to remember to cancel. Then I thought about all the questions she'd asked. Maybe it would be helpful to meet one more time.

"I have one more question for you to spend some serious time considering until we meet again." She gave me a serious look. "What is your heart's desire?"

I felt a flutter in my chest. It had been a long time since I'd even come close to thinking about my heart's desire. I said a noncommittal, "Hmm," and changed the subject. "I can still use the SPM discount, right?"

"Sure can," she said cheerfully. "That's why we have it."

I quickly wrote a check so I could switch gears to asking about Twila, but then I noticed a binder on her desk with a large gold label that said Merritt Finance Consulting. "Is that Bert Merritt's company?"

"Yes, why?"

"My dad has some money with him," I said. "Sharon asked if I wanted to invest when I first met her, but I'm still at the point where I put all of my money into the business."

"That's good business sense," she said. "But I am earning quite a chunk of change with them."

"Could I take a look at that?" I asked. "Maybe I could squeeze some money out in the next couple of months if it makes sense."

She put her hand down on the binder. "Oh, I'm sorry. This one is personalized for me. It has my financial info in it. I shouldn't have left it on the desk."

"No problem." I moved toward the door.

"All you have to do is talk to Bert. I'm sure he'd be happy to create one for you," she said. "He's great at explaining all of those financial terms too. Oh, and if you do sign up with him, please let him know I referred you. Then I get a finder's fee."

"Sure," I said.

"Oh wait," she said. "I think they're having one of those dinners where they tell you all about their funds. I'll look for it and email you an invite."

Sharon and Bert were both somewhat overzealous in their marketing, and I didn't want to tell Fawn that I'd tagged their emails as Spam, so I never saw them anymore.

"Thanks. I appreciate that." I paused on the way to the door. "So terrible about Twila." Not the best segue, but it was all I could come up with.

"Awful," she said.

"Were you close to her?" I asked. "It's just, I can't imagine anyone disliking her enough to..."

She opened her mouth and closed it, and then opened the door.

Was she about to tell me someone who didn't like Twila? "I'm sorry." I took a step through and stopped, turning to block her in. "I wasn't trying to make you break life coach confidentiality or anything."

"Of course not," she said. "You wouldn't want me to blab about your personal business to my other clients."

Wait. Did that mean one of her clients didn't like Twila? "It's just that I haven't met anyone who had a problem with Twila," I said.

She raised her eyebrows.

"Really? Someone did?" I asked. "I can't imagine."

She stayed quiet. I wasn't getting anywhere. Maybe I should ask a more pointed question.

"Do you have a confidentiality problem with being her website administrator?" That came out more exasperated than I planned.

She laughed. "No."

"Because you had mentioned at the SPM meeting that the website was getting a lot of hits, so I wondered if there was anything, I don't know, suspicious on Twila's site."

She shook her head. "Nothing suspicious. She had this one guy who was a bit obsessed with her puzzles. He complained anytime he could find more than one answer."

"Oh," I said. "Did you tell the police about him?"

She frowned. "No. Do you think I should?"

"They asked me to tell them anything and everything," I said. "Do you know the guy's name?"

"Oh yeah. Tod Walker." Her tone of voice made him seem like a big problem.

"That bad, huh?" I said sympathetically. "Maybe he needs your life coach help."

"He needs some kind of help, that's for sure. He took puzzles way too seriously," she said. "Why are you asking about him?"

"I can't help but be curious about all of this." Time to distract her. "Could I check out your garage? My dad could use some help in his."

"Sure, a quick look," she said. "I have another appointment coming soon, but I love to show it off."

We went through her house and peeked in. Sharon had created overhead storage with metal racks and neatly labeled clear plastic boxes. She'd also lined one wall with shelves similar to those in Fawn's office, this time filled with various brightly colored fabric boxes that had lids.

"It's so organized," I said. "Is it hard to keep it that way?"

"Well, Sharon provided some training that I use to help me keep up with it," she said. "I juggle a lot of jobs, and every bit helps."

Then I remembered the other question I was asking the SPM members and pulled out the Lice Club Lady card. "Hey, I've asked some of the other moms about these cards I saw at the trade show. Do you know who this is?"

"I think I know why you're asking all these questions," she said. "You're really just trying to make sense of Twila's death. And perhaps death in general. We should focus on that in our next session."

* * * *

I sent an email to Lani about Tod Walker and Sharon's unlikely suggestion of people on the housing waiting list, and then I realized I was very close to Mona's house. Maybe I could pop in and ask her about her products, and hint that I'd be having a hot date sometime soon. I thought about Joss sitting on my dad's couch, his T-shirt tightening across his chest. And Joss walking across the farm in his gray tank top. And Joss—

I gave myself a time out, taking a deep breath to get the lust out of my system. It didn't work. Pulling in front of Mona's house, I mentally debated if this impulse was a good idea, and then forced myself to get out of the car. She probably wouldn't even be home.

I knocked on her front door, nervous as hell, and heard her say in a low sexy voice, "Just a minute."

Her house was almost a clone of Fawn's, although Mona had bucked tradition and painted her house the lightest shade of pink. The rest of the street was solidly off white. Was that incense I smelled from inside? Who the heck used incense these days?

Mona opened the door with a dramatic flourish and squealed when she saw that it was me. She slammed the door in my face. "What are you doing here?" she squawked, pretty much the opposite of a sultry voice.

It was easy to see why she was upset. She'd been wearing a red silk teddy with black lace and a matching thigh length robe. She was definitely not expecting me.

"I'm so sorry!" I said. "I'll come back another time, I mean, I'll call first or something."

"Go. Away. Now."

"I'm gone!" I said, trying not to laugh as the humor of the situation came over me. I walked to my car, wondering who she'd been expecting. Then I moved a little slower. Maybe I should hang around and find out. Wouldn't a real investigator do just that?

In case she was watching me, I got in my car, pulled out, and drove around the block. I parked a few doors away, and waited. It didn't take long for her real guest to arrive. A BMW rocketed into her driveway, and a man in a very nice suit got out. I didn't recognize him.

I pulled my phone out, zoomed in, and took a few photos, hoping I was able to catch enough of his face to ask Lani if she recognized him. From my vantage point, I couldn't see if she let him in, but he didn't return to his car for the whole ten minutes I forced myself to wait before heading home.

I drove by her house slowly. The door was closed. Unless he was some kind of magician, she'd let him in.

But who was he? And why was she wearing lingerie to greet him?

* * * *

I had two hours to spend on the proposal before I needed to leave to get Elliott from camp. Since I didn't know how the pick-up process worked, and I wanted to avoid those elementary school moms who were ruthless about getting a front place in line, I planned to leave early and work in the car while I waited.

Elliott must be having a great time. He hadn't texted me since the morning, other than a *Yes!* with a happy face emoji in response to a *Going well?* text from me.

"I figured out something," my dad said as soon as I came in. He was sitting at the makeshift desk in the living room, looking more energetic than I'd seen him in a while.

Trouble turned her head from her perch on the back of the couch where she'd been looking out the window. "Meow," she said. *Ignore him and come and see these nasty, good-for-nothing squirrels out there.*

"About what?" I said.

"Your bad review," he said. "Look. The same guy wrote a bunch of bad reviews on almost all the organic pet food companies in California and Nevada."

"Wow! How'd you figure that out?"

"He really likes using Spanish words for colors as his last name. Grana, Oro, Blanco. But he reuses the same phrases," he explained. "In ten of these he mentioned 'chemical smell' and in a bunch of others he used the phrase 'smelled awful.'"

When I didn't respond, he said. "If you read all of them, you'd see the pattern too."

"Oh, I believe you," I said, getting angry. "What do we do?"

"I asked one of my buddies to look into it," he said.

"Your buddy?"

"Yeah, he took some class on how to outwit hackers," he said. "It was more like a how to hack class."

I had created a monster. "One class and he can hack into SDHelp?"

"He's not going to hack in," he said.

"That's good," I said. "We don't need any more trouble with the police."

"He's going to ask someone who can." He seemed really happy with himself.

"Wait, what?"

"Besides, he's with the police," he said.

I shook my head. "I'm so confused. He's a police officer and he's helping you hack?"

"Not an officer," he said. "He works at the station."

"Won't he get in trouble?" Or could *we* get in trouble?

He shrugged. "I don't think so. The way he tells it, they can't get by without him."

"I don't want him to lose his job over this," I said.

He waved his hand. "Nah. It's all good."

Trouble meowed again. It sounded like a warning to me.

* * * *

"We already learned the first three songs!" Elliott said as soon as he got in the car. A bunch of kids waved good-bye to him, which warmed my heart.

"Nice!" I pulled out slowly, watching out for wayward theater kids.

He went on excitedly talking about the dance moves, blocking, and how he knew more lines than anyone else.

"Do you like the director?" I asked.

"He worked with all the little kids today," Elliott said. "All of us principals worked with the assistant director, Larry."

I could tell he really liked being one of the "principals."

"Seems like you're making friends already," I said.

"Yeah. It was weird at first not knowing everyone, but then it was okay." He paused. "Maybe when I'm done, it might be weird going back to my old group."

Shoot. I hadn't thought about that. "Well, now you'll know even more people in theater." I tried for cheerful but went a little overboard.

He nodded, picking at a small tear in the edge of the seat. "We are moving back, right?"

I couldn't tell what he was trying to ask me. "Do you want to stay?"

He looked at me and then out the window. "Maybe," he said. "I don't know. I like seeing Grandpa all the time. And I like having a whole house. And yard. And I like Annie, and Joss, and the chicks. But I miss my friends."

"What about school in the fall?" I kept my voice noncommittal, not at all sure what I wanted myself.

"Yeah, a new school would be really weird," he said. "But that other guy who tried out for Horton said the middle school uses the real theater at the high school for their plays, and had all the same sets and stuff. It could be cool."

I didn't push it any further. I couldn't think beyond my big meeting the next day with the business consultant, my potential deal with Twomey's, and my dad getting healthy again, not in that order. Then I'd deal with all of these decisions.

* * * *

After dinner, Elliott got another guitar lesson and I called Lani to get a boost of self-confidence her enthusiasm always gave me.

"Hey, future business mogul," she said. "Ready for your big day?"

I could hear hissing in the background. "What's that noise?"

"I'm spray painting about a mile of silk. It's a special order. A bride's dress." She sounded a little distracted.

"Really?" I imagined the adorable, but cartoon quality of her regular designs. "Who is it? What are you painting on it?"

"I can't tell you her name, but an actress wants her twin toddlers to be her attendants and wants their skirts to match the skirt of her wedding dress. I think the little girls picked this smiling sun design from an outfit I made last year."

"I guess the tangerine giraffes were too much for a wedding," I said.

"It's not my job to judge," Lani said. "Especially with the amount she's paying me."

"Whoa," I said, thinking what yards of Lani's work went for. "Didn't think about that."

"You okay?" she asked.

I told her about the new SDHelp reviews and what my dad had figured out. "What if it affects Twomey's decision?"

The hissing stopped. "That's terrible. Can you contact SDHelp and ask to have them taken down?"

"There's no way to contact anyone," I said. "They just post guidelines on how to handle negative reviews."

"Can you see who posted it?" she asked.

"No," I said. "It just says 'G. Verde' in Encinitas. And that's after 'J. Greene' last week." I told her about the use of colors in most of the names.

"Hold on," she said. "I want to look at it online."

I waited for her to find her laptop and check out the review, while Trouble sat in my lap, purring.

"The first bad review was posted right before Twila's murder," she said. "And this one mentions that you're a suspect. Why would someone be that awful?" she said. "Uh-oh. What if this G. Verde guy killed Twila?"

"Lani," I said. "How long have you been working with that spray paint?"

"Since six," she said.

"This morning?" I asked. "Where's Piper?"

"At that conference in Anaheim I told you about," she said. "And I'm fine. I'm just sitting here."

"Turn off that machine and go outside for some fresh air," I said in my mom tone. "Call me in the morning and we'll talk about this then."

"No," she said.

"Get away from those paint fumes now or I'm calling Piper," I said, only slightly kidding.

"You wouldn't," she said.

"You know I would," I said. "Now get going."

"Okay," she said like a sulky child. "But only because I can't see straight."

* * * *

I forced myself to go to sleep at midnight, my eyes feeling sticky from going over my proposal, sure that all the spreadsheets and marketing ideas were pipe dreams.

Zoey was handling all the Meowio Batali cooking this morning so I could focus on the meeting with Quincy Powell, businessman extraordinaire, according to Lani. I printed out the entire document, fighting my dad's printer when it jammed, but finally getting a nice copy and putting it in a thin binder.

I dressed in my most business-like outfit, black pants that made me sweat as soon as I put them on, and a light blue button-down shirt. I tossed a black suit jacket over my arm, but couldn't bear the thought of wearing it in this heat. Maybe if I got to air conditioning.

My dad wished me good luck, and I was on my way. I followed my GPS to an industrial area of Kearny Mesa and pulled into the parking lot of the El Cajon Rental Kitchen.

Quincy Powell was pacing back and forth in front of the building talking emphatically into a cell phone and gesturing with his other arm. He was a tall African-American man with gray hair and a gray goatee, wearing a silk short-sleeved shirt over charcoal gray jeans and red boat shoes.

As soon as he saw me drive in, he stopped his conversation, tucked his phone in his pants pocket, and walked over to meet me. "Colbie, I presume," he said. "Nice to meet you."

I almost dropped the shoulder bag holding my laptop and the proposal as I got out of the car. "Thanks so much for taking the time to meet with me."

"Of course," he said. "Lani has told me so much about you."

"Only the good stuff, I assume." I said, and he laughed good-naturedly.

"Let's take a look inside and then we can go over your numbers," he said, twirling the set of keys around on his finger. I got the impression that he was rarely still.

"Sounds great," I said as I fell into step beside him. "Lani says you've helped her a lot."

"Aw shucks," he said, making fun of himself. "She's a real go-getter. She didn't really need me." He unlocked the door. "I'll give you the five dollar tour," he said and then stuck out his foot. "As soon as you tell me what you think of these shoes." The impish look in his eyes made him look younger.

"Um," I said. "Cool?"

"You sure?" He turned his foot sideways as if checking them out. "I took my granddaughter shopping and she insisted I try them on. They were so comfortable that I bought them, but the color is a bit much for me." He shook his head.

"They're not you?" I asked. "I think Lani would approve though."

"That she would." He opened the door and gestured for me to go in.

We entered a wide hall that led to two doors. The smell of baked goods hung in the air. "Yum," I said.

"Yeah," he said. "The bakers are here all night." He paused outside a set of double doors. "Lani said you were outgrowing your other current workspace, so I thought you'd want to check this out."

He opened one of the doors, and the sounds of a busy kitchen hit us.

"Yo, Quincy," said a burly man using a wooden spoon as big as a paddle to mix a cauldron-sized pot. A baker's staff was putting sprinkles on chocolate cups that would probably hold something delicious like mousse, and another group had a complicated sandwich assembly line going.

The room was huge, with four double-ovens, four stove tops holding six burners each, four sinks, one of which could hold all my pans at one time and more, refrigerators, freezers, and an acre of stainless steel tables in the center of the room. Only a quarter of it was being used.

"Wow," I said.

He opened the closest refrigerator, each shelf labeled with the owner of the food. It was so big, I could practically live in it.

"There's also a store room through there for dry goods," he said.

"It's pretty amazing," I said. "How much?"

"Less than you might imagine," he said. "How about we go over some numbers?" He showed me to an office in the back.

"You work here?" I asked. It didn't look like a business tycoon's office with its ancient desk and beat up metal file cabinet. We sat down at a small table. At least the chairs were comfortable.

"Once in a while," he said. He reached for the proposal I'd pulled out of my bag. "Nice." He put on reading glasses and read quickly.

I pulled out my laptop, and he asked, "Can you bring up the spreadsheets?"

He peered at the first one and then asked. "May I?"

At my nod, he started clicking back and forth between the accompanying spreadsheets, deep in concentration.

I sat quietly, my hands shaking.

"This organic seafood is significantly more expensive than regular," he said, without looking up from the numbers. "Is that necessary? Maybe you could sell one or two products that aren't organic."

"No, I couldn't," I said. "My whole brand is organic. And human grade. I'm not going to change that to save money."

He nodded. "How did you build your supply chain? Will they be able to handle an increase in demand from you?"

I'd wondered the same thing. "I looked into that. Only about half said they'd be able to double my demand. I'd have to find new suppliers."

"You use specialty products, so it's not so easy." He frowned at the computer. "Is it okay if I start a new spreadsheet and work some numbers?"

"Sure," I said.

He started typing away, copying numbers from my spreadsheet and putting them into his.

He turned the laptop to face me and pointed to a figure. "Here," he said. "That could be your profit if you get the Twomey's deal and expand."

The number was four times what I cleared in a year. And that was just year one.

Chapter 13

I arrived at home, energized by my meeting with Quincy, who had not only helped to rework my business proposal for Twomey's but also recommended I look into a small business loan to pay for the additional staff and other expenses. He'd offered discounted use of his kitchen, just one of the businesses he ran that were incubators for new companies, and access to his food supply chain, which offered bulk discounts I couldn't get on my own. The savings would be significant.

I'd come very close to agreeing to a deal with him for Powell Ventures to become a minority investor. An investor. During tough times, I'd dreamed of having an angel investor shower me with money so I could grow my business with less worry. Why was I balking now?

My dad had texted me that he was going out to lunch with Annie, and Lani had sent me several texts asking how the meeting went. But I wanted to go over Quincy's numbers and gather my thoughts before calling her back.

He'd asked me some questions that were similar to Fawn's life coach questions. *What kind of success was I looking for? What was the next step beyond selling my products at Twomey's?*

I'd never even considered what happened after. A regular contract with Twomey's would mean a steady income that wasn't at the mercy of farmers' market attendance, or weather, or website orders. It meant stability. And growth, where I'd be able to hire more people to help me cook and handle some of the business aspects.

But deep inside was the smallest hint of a dream. Meowio products in pet stores across the country.

Then Quincy had asked me the killer question. *If I had all the resources I could imagine, what did I truly want my business to be?*

I wasn't one for introspection. I didn't have the time or energy. But in two days, I'd been forced to think about all kinds of things.

I pulled into the driveway and saw a familiar feathered friend on the porch. Charlie. He came to the edge of the porch and peeked around the railing, and then went back to pushing the doorbell.

I walked up the stairs to the sound of "Yankee Doodle" clamoring inside the house. "Hey, Charlie."

Trouble sat on the kitchen windowsill, her growl coming through the window with her eyes fixated on the bird. Charlie must have figured out that she couldn't get to him, because he ignored her, pushing the button and tilting his head as if listening to the tune.

"Time to go home, kid," I said and shooed him off the porch with my hands.

Charlie went without protest, seeming quite happy to be heading home. I followed him as he puttered along the sidewalk and hopped right up on the front porch. I even let him ring the doorbell.

Joss opened the door and smiled. "I think my bird has a thing for you."

I caught my breath. That was definitely flirting. "Maybe I have a thing for..." I paused, "Him."

His face flushed a little. "Um."

"Um." I smiled. "How are the chicks doing?"

He blew out a breath. "Good. Want to see them?"

"Sure."

He held out his hand, inviting me to go down the steps first. "You're all dressed up."

"I had a meeting with a potential investor," I said, just as Charlie dove in front of me. I stopped short and Joss almost ran into me, grabbing my arms right above my elbows.

We both stood there for a second, before he realized how close he was. He cleared his throat and took a step back. "How did that go?"

If I didn't know better, I'd say that Charlie was totally matchmaking. "It was... really interesting." I gave him some highlights of the meeting while he held the gate for me and we walked into the pen. I stopped, remembering my flip flop disaster. "Maybe I should put my rain boots on."

He laughed. "Afraid of some dirt?"

"Just chicken poop," I said but followed him through the coop and into the small incubator room.

The chicks gave a chorus of chirps. "They've grown already," I said, surprised.

"It happens fast," Joss agreed. He picked one up and put it in my hand. This time his hand brushed mine, and I looked up at him.

I felt a zing. And from the look in his eyes, he did too.

It had been a long time but I knew what to do. I leaned forward at the same time he did and we kissed.

It was light and sweet but definitely a kiss. He stepped back, looking a bit dazed.

"Whoa," I said, smiling.

"Whoa," he agreed, but his smile became strained.

He did not seem happy about the kiss. What the heck? I struggled not to feel hurt and acted cool. "So, what are you going to do with these chicks?"

"Sell them as soon as they're old enough." He sounded regretful.

"Who buys them?"

"Some will go as pets but most will be egg layers," he said. "All but two are female. Their blue eggs go for more money."

"That's something our businesses have in common," I said. "We have specialty items that customers are willing to pay more money for."

"True," he said. "I thought my organic subscription service would be doing better. Right now I'm filling about forty boxes a month."

"Have you tried the farmers' markets?" I asked.

"Not here," he said. "Maybe when I can hire someone to handle it for me."

I raised the chick to my face. "Will it be hard to let these little guys go?"

"A little," he admitted. "I've been a farmer most of my life, so I know the deal." He picked up another chick and petted its head with one gentle finger.

"Elliott said you moved here from Alaska because of your daughter," I said, hoping I didn't sound nosy.

He frowned. "Yeah. It's kind of messy right now. My ex got some judge to say it was too dangerous for Kai, that's my daughter's name, to come and visit my farm in Alaska. So I called her bluff and moved down here. Still fighting to share custody."

"That's too bad." I thought about Elliott hoping to meet his biological dad and felt a twinge of regret. Maybe I should've encouraged it earlier.

"Kai and I used to have a great time on the farm. She'd come for a month in the summer," he said. "She's barely been here."

"That's a shame," I said. "She must love these little guys."

He nodded, putting the chick back.

"I really hope it works out," I said. "I better get back. I know my dad wants to hear about my appointment." I tipped the chick into his hands. "Thanks for letting me see the chicks again."

"You're welcome anytime." He held the door, but kept back far enough that I didn't brush up against him.

Which totally made me want to, but I held myself back. I wasn't going to throw myself at the man, for heaven's sake. He walked me out of the pen in silence.

"Okay, well, bye," I said at the gate.

"Bye." He closed the gate, with him on the other side. "Good luck with that business dude."

"Thanks." I went over the kiss the whole way back. Obviously, he didn't feel the same way I did about it. Or maybe I shouldn't have brought up his daughter. "Okay, I can deal with that. What's a little awkwardness between neighbors?" I said out loud.

* * * *

Trouble had calmed down by the time I got home, purring and winding around my ankles as if thanking me for getting rid of the intruder on her porch. My dad texted me that Annie was taking him to his favorite Irish pub after lunch, where a bunch of his Boston buddies liked to hang out. I was happy that he was feeling well enough to be out and about.

Lani didn't answer her phone, so I left her a long message about the meeting with Quincy. Then I spent some time evaluating his spreadsheets and making some changes to my proposal for Twomey's.

Picking up Elliott from his musical theater programs had always been a fun part of my day. I knew he'd fit right in with all the theater kids, and that he'd love the backstage interactions. He generally avoided the drama that occurred in any group, let alone drama kids, but he liked to report it all to me.

"We learned all the way through 'All the Things You Can Think'." He pulled his notebook out of his *Wicked* backpack and paged through it. "And tomorrow, we're practicing 'Alone in the Universe' with the voice coach."

"Nice!" I pulled into What's the Scoop? Ice Cream.

Elliott looked up to see why we'd stopped. "Awesome! Can I get two scoops?"

I laughed. "Don't you always?"

Lani called me back, and I handed Elliott money. "Can you get me my usual?"

"Sure," he said with pretend exasperation. Then he changed his tune. "Chocolate dipped in a cherry shell coming right up."

"Hi, Lani." I watched Elliott walk up to the outside window and turned around to focus.

"I got your message," she said. "I told you Quincy was awesome."

"He seems to be," I said. We talked more about the meeting. "I'm making the changes he suggested to the Twomey's proposal and will send it in. Maybe even tonight." I turned around to check on Elliott. A tall, bald man was looming over him. "Shit. Gotta go."

I hung up the phone and ran over to them, dodging a dad leaving with his son on his shoulders. Elliott clutched his two ice cream cones, looking up with wide eyes. When he saw me coming, he looked even more scared.

"What are you doing?" I demanded of the man.

"No problem here," the man said. His face was expressionless behind his mirrored sunglasses but still seemed menacing.

"Are you okay?" I grabbed Elliott by the shoulders and he appeared unhurt, just frightened. I turned back to the man and got in his face. "Why are you scaring my kid?"

The man took a step back and gave a scoffing laugh. He tossed his ice cream in the garbage can. Somehow that was even more intimidating. "I think we understand each other." He walked toward the street.

I moved to follow him and Elliott yelled, "No, Mom!" He waited for the jerk to jog across the street and disappear down an alley.

"What happened?" I asked.

"He said…" Elliott started and stopped, his voice rising with worry. "He said that I had a nosy mom and that if she doesn't stop asking questions…" He stared after him.

"What?" I felt my insides quiver.

"If she doesn't stop asking questions, she's going to be in big trouble!"

* * * *

Annie was pulling her car into her driveway just as we arrived at the house. My dad got out slowly with a pained expression on his face. Maybe visiting the pub had been too much for him.

"Don't say anything to Grandpa," I told Elliott. We had taken the time to calm down and eat our dripping cones in the car before heading home. Then I saw my dad almost stumble. "Why don't you go see the chicks and I'll figure out what to tell him."

Elliott's face brightened and he hurried toward the farm. I watched him go, wondering if I had to worry about him in our own neighborhood.

"Colbie!" Annie seemed delighted to see me. She wore a sleeveless flowered shirt and green baseball cap with "Seize the Day" in pink crystals. "We had the nicest lunch at Pico's. He said to say 'hi', of course."

My dad handed me a to-go package. "Got a bunch of chicken tacos for dinner." His smile was forced. "The bartender at the pub put 'em in the fridge for you."

"Yum!" I said, taking the package and holding his arm. "Thanks so much, Annie. I'll see you later." I steered my dad down the short driveway. The fact that he didn't try to pull away was alarming, especially the way he started wheezing as we walked up our porch steps. A coughing spell caused him to stop on the second step.

"How are those lungs?" I asked.

He just shook his head. Inside, he held onto the wall until he made it to his chair. I got him a whiskey and he sipped it, then took a hit of his inhaler. His breathing eased.

"Overdid it a bit, I see." I sat down on the couch. Trouble watched from the doorway before jumping on to the couch. She stared at my dad, her tail twitching.

He nodded, still not trusting his voice.

"So I get to do all the talking," I joked, my voice a little unsteady with worry. I told him about my meeting with Quincy while keeping an eye on him.

"Sounds good," he said. "Where's that kitchen again?"

"Kearny Mesa," I said. "A little closer to here." My cell phone rang again. Shoot! I'd forgotten to call Lani back after Elliott's run in with the nasty guy. "Is it okay if I update Lani? I know she's dying of curiosity."

"Sure," he said, waving me away.

I took the phone into the kitchen to tell Lani what happened to Elliott, keeping my voice low so my dad couldn't hear.

"Oh my God," she said. "Someone knows you're investigating."

"Obviously the wrong person," I said.

"He must have followed you to the ice cream shop," she said. "Did you notice anyone behind you?"

"No. But I wasn't really looking."

"Who have you talked to lately?" she asked. "Who knows that you're looking into this?"

I told her about Fawn and Mona.

"I know it's not Fawn," she said, and I didn't call her on her blind faith in her friend. "But maybe she told someone."

We were both silent. She was probably going through all the different possibilities, like I'd been doing since it happened.

"You have to tell your detective about him," she said finally. "Maybe she can figure out who he is. From security cameras or something."

I didn't say anything.

"Colbie." Her voice was serious. "Keeping Elliott and you safe is the most important thing."

"I'm sure Norma's not going to be happy about me asking questions," I said.

"She also won't be happy if she hears it from me first," she threatened.

"Okay, fine," I said. "I'll call her. But first, is Piper home from her conference?"

"Yes," she said. "She's right here."

"Any chance you guys can stop by?" My throat closed up with worry and I had to grab a glass of water from the sink.

"Both of us?" she asked. "What's up?"

I took a sip before answering. "My dad's cough was getting better, but today it seems much worse. He has a doctor's visit scheduled for Thursday. I think he's trying to hold out until then, but…"

"We'll be right over," Lani said.

"That'd be great." I felt the tension in my neck subside, just a bit. My dad really liked Piper. Maybe he'd listen to her if she told him to go to the doctor before Thursday.

I peeked in on my dad, and saw him sleeping, with Trouble continuing to keep watch over him. I busied myself in the kitchen until I heard a knock on the door. Lani knew how much I disliked the "Yankee Doodle" doorbell so it had to be her.

Piper came in with Lani, her long black hair pulled back into a thick braid. She towered over me and had to bend down to give me a hug. "Where's my favorite cat in the whole wide world?"

Trouble came to meet her, meowing. *I'm everyone's favorite cat.* Then she stuck her butt in the air and stretched before jumping down to wind around Piper's ankle. Piper picked her up and held her like a baby, just the way Trouble liked, smooching the cat's face with noisy kisses.

"What can I get you?" I asked. "We have wine, beer, and all kinds of soda."

"Tea would be great," Piper said.

"Me too," Lani said. They headed into the living room.

"How's it going, Hank?" Lani asked.

"Can't complain," he said, but started a bout of coughing.

By the time I delivered their tea, they'd been brought up to date on Elliott's play and were talking about my new opportunity.

"Elliott will be back soon," I said. "Do you guys want to stay for dinner?"

"We can't," Lani said. "I have to get my project out. But thanks."

My dad took a sip of whiskey, but the cough still wracked his body.

Piper moved to sit closer to my dad. "Ooh, that sounds bad, Mr. Summers." Her dark eyes showed her concern.

"Hank," he said, in between coughs.

"Hank," she corrected herself. "I have my bag in the car. How about if I take a listen to those lungs?"

"That's a great idea," I said, ignoring my dad's head shake.

He frowned at me, and then Lani helped me to tag-team him. "Oh you know Piper, Hank," she said. "She won't take no for an answer. Hey, what is going on with that Red Sox bench?"

He snorted in disgust. "They're really losing it lately."

Piper was back in a few minutes.

"Hey, Lani," I said. "I wanted to show you Quincy's spreadsheets." We went into the kitchen to give Piper and my dad some privacy.

"Can you hear anything?" Lani whispered, neither one of us pretending to look at the laptop.

I shook my head. Even on the side of the kitchen closest to the living room, I could only hear Piper's professional murmurs.

"Where's Elliott?" she asked, still whispering.

"At Joss's," I said, wondering if, or when, I should tell her about flirting. And the kiss. It didn't seem appropriate now.

Piper stuck her head out of the living room, catching us in the kitchen doorway. "Colbie? I'm kidnapping your dad for a bit, okay?"

"Um, okay," I said.

"I'm going to ask a favor of a friend and get him a breathing treatment this afternoon," she said. "Should do the trick." She paused. "I hope that's okay."

"That's great," I said. "Right, Dad? No waiting."

He didn't even argue. That combined with the concern on Piper's face had my heart quivering.

Piper and Lani did some kind of silent couple communication and Lani said, "Why don't I take my favorite twelve-year-old to our house for a while? That way you can tag along with your dad."

I took a moment to think of anything I had to tell her, and she insisted. "Elliott will be fine. You go along with Piper, and I'll spoil your kid rotten before you both get home."

I did as I was told, gathering up my purse, and at the last minute, my laptop and charger. I had a feeling it was going to be a long night.

Chapter 14

Piper stayed with us while the emergency room doctor explained that my dad's x-rays showed an infection that was triggering his asthma, and that he'd be admitted to the hospital as soon as they arranged for a room.

Piper must have known that would happen, which was why she'd pushed my dad to come in.

He wasn't even mad, just exhausted. Maybe even relieved. He was given a breathing treatment and put on oxygen. As soon as he started breathing easier, he fell into a fitful sleep, even with all the noise going on around our little curtained off area. I sat in the chair beside the bed, feeling terrible. I'd thought he was doing better, but I must have missed something.

Soon, they were transferring him to another bed where they were going to transport him to his room. I was asked to leave so they could settle him in, so I called Lani from the sitting lounge to tell her what was happening. She'd already been texting with Piper and had arranged for Elliott to stay overnight with Annie. And she was happy to take him to camp the next morning.

Piper came to tell me that I could go up to my dad's room. "He'll be well taken care of." She had early morning rounds the next day so she headed home.

My dad was propped up with the bed angled high and a bunch of supporting pillows to help his breathing. He was attached by wires to beeping machines and had an oxygen mask over his nose and mouth. The nurse bustled about and let me know that his lungs were already improving.

I put the TV on for him, but he kept dozing off. He didn't seem up for talking.

A wave of deep remorse washed over me. What if he didn't get better? I regretted how much I'd rebelled against him when I was eighteen. I couldn't imagine if Elliott dropped out of my life like I'd done to my dad. Now I could admit that deep down I always knew I could go home. I was just too stubborn to admit I was wrong.

Was it too late to make up for those years? And did Elliott's father have any of the same regrets?

* * * *

After dinner, Lani brought Elliott to visit but my dad was sleeping again. I stepped out into the hallway.

"He's doing better," I assured Elliott.

His face was pinched with worry. "Are you sure?"

"Yes, I'm sure." I held up my little finger. "Pinky swear."

He held up his pinky to shake and gave me a brief smile, but it was for my benefit.

"He'll be sad he missed you," I said. "You're okay with staying at Annie's tonight, right? I'm sure Lani will bring you something gooey for breakfast if I can't take you to camp."

"Maybe I shouldn't go," he said.

I paused. "That's really nice of you to offer, but if Grandpa needs anything, I'm here for him. He's already improving. Pretty soon, he'll be home and playing guitar with you."

* * * *

My dad and I were both bleary-eyed and cranky the next morning when a new nurse cheerfully bustled in. "You should get some breakfast, dear, while I take care of my patient."

I stumbled down to the surprisingly nice cafeteria and poured myself a vat of coffee. It must have been some special kind of high octane because it jolted me awake enough to figure out that I was starving. I devoured a cheese omelet, hash browns, and a warm orange-cranberry muffin before grabbing another cup of coffee to go.

My dad was sitting up when I arrived, still attached to a bunch of machines. He'd been pushing around some scrambled eggs, but put down his fork and leaned back against the pillows when he saw me.

"Not hungry?" I asked.

He shook his head. "You don't have to stay with me."

I tried not to feel hurt. "I'm good. Unless you…" *Don't want me here…* "Want to be alone."

He cleared his throat. "I'm just…"

I waited.

"I never wanted you to see me like this," he admitted, keeping his eyes down.

I took a minute to catch my breath. "How many times did you take care of me when I was sick?"

"That's different," he said.

"I have Elliott," I said. "I know how that feels. But someday he's going to need to take care of me. That's just the way the world works."

His hands moved restlessly on the white sheets. "I'm really sick of being sick," he admitted.

"I know." I had to blink back tears. "That's why you're here. To get better."

His shoulders relaxed a little and he closed his eyes.

"Hey," I said. "They have salt water taffy in the gift shop. I know it's your favorite. How about I get us some?"

He opened his eyes and smiled.

* * * *

Annie came to visit my dad as soon as Lani picked up Elliott for camp. "He's fine," she told me. "He slept really well and had a good breakfast. Such a wonderful young man."

Which of course made me smile.

"You go on home and take care of what you need to take care of," she said. "I cleared my morning so don't rush back."

I took her advice and went home to shower and change. Trouble yowled at me the second I walked in the door. *Where were you? I was here all night by myself!* I picked her up and cradled her until she calmed down. Elliott had given her food—Seafood Surprise—and fresh water. He really was a wonderful young man.

I sat at the kitchen table and pulled out my phone. I'd received texts galore from Lani. *How's your dad? How are you? Make sure you call the detective! And lock your doors! I couldn't sleep last night worrying about that big bald man. You don't know what he's really up to.*

She was going to make someone a great mother someday. Even though the texts made me feel a little rebellious (was that what my nagging did to Elliott?), I dialed Norma's number.

"Detective Chiron," she said in an *I'm busy so this better be important* tone.

"Hi, Detective," I said. "Colbie Summers here."

"What can I do for you?"

I could hear a lot of voices in the background and imagined her in a police station like on TV. "I had an incident yesterday that I think I should tell you about." I told her what the tall bald man had said to Elliott.

"Can you describe him?" she asked.

I closed my eyes to jog my memory. "Um, over six feet. Bald. Wearing a brown short sleeved shirt and beige khakis." Should I add surly and mean?

"What questions was he talking about?" she asked.

Uh-oh. I was too tired to think of a good excuse. "I have no idea." I sounded defensive even to myself.

She didn't say anything, employing that old police trick of leaving room for the guilty party to speak and hang themselves.

"I may have asked one of the SPM moms a question about Twila," I admitted, beginning to sweat. If I was in an interrogation room, I'd have folded like a cheap suit. Or an accordion. Or one of those origami swans.

She stayed silent.

"Or two." I held my breath to stop myself from saying more.

Finally she spoke. "Two moms or two questions?"

I waited as long as I could stand it. "Moms."

She didn't say anything.

"Or three. Moms." I was like a kid confessing to a parent. It made me feel marginally better to relieve the guilt, but then I worried what punishment I'd have to face. But really, what could she do to me?

"You say this happened yesterday." She didn't sound angry, just curious. "Why didn't you call before now?"

Now *that* I had an answer to. I explained about my dad and she said all the right things and then returned to the subject at hand. "Any chance you could stop by and meet with a sketch artist? And have Elliott come by as well?"

I paused. He shouldn't have to deal with this stress on top of my dad's illness. "I can be there this morning, but Elliott is at camp."

"We could have the artist stop by—"

I interrupted her. "No. I don't want him bothered."

She waited but this time I didn't try to appease her.

"I have some business stuff to take care of, and then I'll come to the station," I said, trying to take some control of the situation. "What's the address?"

She gave me directions and then added, "We can talk about the penalties for obstruction of justice when you get here."

She hung up.

* * * *

An hour later, I'd made any changes I could think of to my business proposal. I held my breath and hit *Send*, with a mixture of excitement and terror. I'd done my best. Now I just had to wait.

Trouble sat on her windowsill, surveying her kingdom. She turned and meowed. *Good job.*

"Thank you," I said, as if I could understand her. "It'll work out." I told myself out loud. Except sometimes it didn't.

She meowed again. *Get to the police station.*

"So now you're channeling Lani," I joked.

My phone lit up with a Facebook notification. Maybe just a bit of procrastinating. I clicked over to the Facebook app and saw a bunch of posts in the private SPM group page. Twila had created a public page for marketing and a private page where we could share information that wasn't for our customers to see.

Sharon had posted a reminder that she was holding an open house of Fawn's garage. It was tomorrow, by invitation only, and we were all invited. We should also let anyone who was interested in Sharon's services to come by and see her work.

If my dad wasn't in the hospital, that open house would be a great opportunity to ask Sharon more questions. But I'd be sticking close to my dad for a while. The investigation would have to wait. As it was, I'd most likely be missing my Thursday afternoon farmers' market the next day. That would cause a hit to my income this month, something I should not be doing with the Twomey's decision looming.

I headed over to the police station and told the officer working at the front desk that I was there to see Detective Chiron. He led me to a conference room and I was surprised to see a young man dressed in a button-down shirt over tan pants show up instead of Norma.

"Hi," he said, tossing down a white sketch pad. "I'm your friendly neighborhood sketch artist."

"Nice to meet you." I sat up in my chair, sure Norma was watching me somehow. The station must be under energy conservation rules. Even though it wasn't as hot as outside, it was way too warm. I was sure my forehead was shiny.

"Relax," he said, as if reading my mind. "This is a conference room. No cameras."

"Sure," I said, stretching it out. "That's not what happens on TV."

He laughed. "Let's get started. Can you describe this guy?"

He did a great job of accurately drawing what I told him. It was a lot harder than I thought it would be to get right; I had to keep the vision in my head from morphing into what he was drawing. And because the guy had been wearing sunglasses, I had no idea of the shape of his eyes. Finally, I decided it was the best I could do.

"Can I get a copy of that to show my son?" I asked. "He might be able to fine tune it."

"Sure," he said. "If you wait here, I'll get it for you." I closed my eyes when he left, trying to fix the guy's face in my memory. It was already a little blurry. Maybe if I saw him again. Of course, I hoped that never happened.

Norma surprised me by bringing back the copy of the drawing herself. "Hello. Can I get you anything before we talk?" She was in the same kind of outfit as before—this time a white jacket over dark jeans.

Ugh. I really didn't want to sit in an interrogation room, no matter what the sketch artist called it. "Um, there's a Philz Coffee down the street. Why don't we go there?"

"We can do that," she said. She led the way out the door and we both put our sunglasses on. A wall of heat hit us. "How's Elliott?"

"He's okay," I said. "Worried about his grandfather, of course." We stayed away from serious talk while we walked down the block and stood in line to place our order. Philz made each cup individually but the wait was worth it.

"Large Julie's Ultimate, creamy." Norma ordered first and stepped to the side. "My treat."

"I'll have the same," I said to the friendly barista with lime green hair. While Norma paid, I looked around the coffee shop for a free table. College kids with laptops were camped out everywhere but once we got our coffees, we found an empty table in the corner. I took a sip and sighed—Philz had the richest coffee in Sunnyside.

She pulled out her notebook. "Why don't you fill me in on what you found out?"

I'd already decided to tell her everything. That Twila had told Daria one of the moms might be doing something unethical. That Gina thought Mona had affairs with married men. That Bronx saw Twila get an upsetting phone call right before she was killed. That Sharon thought people lower on the waiting list for that development might be mad at people at the top, like Twila and Trent. That Fawn told me about Tod Walker complaining on Twila's website.

"So more than a question or two," she said, her face impassive.

"Yes," I admitted.

"Why do people tell you things they don't tell us?" She sounded exasperated. Then she changed her tune and looked me in the eye. "You must stop this and stay out of police business. I'm letting you off the hook about what you've done so far, but if you do something to impede our investigation, I'll have no qualms about throwing you in jail."

I tilted my head, evaluating her expression. "I think you'll have some qualms."

She raised her eyebrows.

"I'm a single mom with a sick dad," I said. "I know there's a heart under all that police toughness."

"Don't try me." She straightened even more in her chair. "I hear you have one of my staff looking into bad reviews of your business."

I blinked. "I don't."

When she gave me a skeptical look, I added, "But I might know someone who did."

She sat back in her chair. "Enlighten me."

"I can't," I said. "But don't you think it's weird that I start getting bad reviews on SDHelp right around the same time…that happened to Twila?"

She didn't say anything but her jaw clenched.

"Did you see that review?" I asked. "The guy who 'wonders where I got my meat'? Don't you think you should find out who that is?"

"We're working on it," she said.

"Oh," I said. "Do you have any, like, leads?"

"No." Her voice was firm. "I didn't say that. I said we're looking into it."

"Okay," I said. I better ask my own questions before we finished our coffee. "Did you ever look into that drug dealer I got evicted?"

"Yes," she said. "He's still in prison. He tried to kill someone in there, so he'll be locked up for a very long time."

"Oh." I tried not to look freaked out. "Good. I think." I took a deep breath and asked the question that had been weighing on my mind. "Am I still a suspect? Officially, I mean."

She looked like she was holding back a smile. "You are officially cleared. Our crime scene experts verified your account of what happened with you and your father that night."

"Really? That's great!" I shook my head. "You couldn't have told me that first?" I decided on another big question. "Can you tell me anything about the phone call Detective Little mentioned?"

That shut her right down. "No." She stood up. "I need to get back."

"Okay," I said. "What about Tod Walker?"

She stopped in her tracks. "You stay away from Todrick Walker. Do you understand me?"

I held up both hands. "Fine. I'm glad you're following up on everyone."

"Yes," she said. "He's not a suspect."

Then my phone rang. It was Elliott. This couldn't be good.

"Mom!" His voice was low but urgent. "That bald man is across the street."

Chapter 15

"What?" I asked, my heart pounding. "Where are you?"

"At camp," Elliott said. "We're eating lunch outside. He's in a black SUV right across the street from the rec center!"

"Hang on." I told Norma what was going on.

She immediately took out her phone and called it in to her station. Then she held out her hand for my cell. "Elliott, this is Detective Norma Chiron. I need you to act like everything is normal. Can you do that? Okay. First, can you get a picture of him? Great. Now find an adult and let them know what's happening. And tell them to behave normally as well. The police are on their way."

"He's leaving!" Elliott's yell was clear as day.

"That's okay." She was in total police mode while I could only feel relief that he was getting away from my son. "Can you see his license plate?"

I couldn't hear his answer, but she looked at me and shook her head. "That's okay. You did perfectly. Here's your mom." She surprised me by taking off at a dead run back the way we'd come.

"Are you okay?" I asked my son, hurrying to catch up to Norma.

"Yeah." Elliott sounded breathless. "I think I can hear a siren. I'm going to find Larry and tell him what happened."

"I'm on my way," I told him.

* * * *

Assistant Director Larry did not appreciate having four Sheriff Department cars converge on the Sunnyside Recreation Center during the camp's lunch break with sirens blasting and lights flashing. Somehow, the SUV made it out of the area, although two other black SUVs *without* tall bald men driving them were stopped and searched.

Norma had one of her technical people working with the photo Elliott had taken to see if it contained any clues that would tell them who the guy was. It was hard to see how well it matched the sketch, even enlarged to show his face.

While everyone was still milling around, I called Annie to see if she could stay a little while longer with my dad. She didn't ask why, just told me to take all the time I needed. I ended up pulling Elliott out of camp early, and bringing him along to visit my dad in the hospital.

"Can we stop at home and get Grandpa's guitar?" Elliott asked.

"Good idea," I said. Maybe the guitar would distract my dad from realizing Elliott was supposed to be at camp.

After stopping for a short time at home, we headed for the hospital. "Hey, kid." I tried to sound calm. "I think the police are getting close to figuring things out, but until they do, I'm going to ask you to be more careful. You can't be anywhere by yourself, okay?"

"Okay." He readily agreed. "Why is that guy following me?"

"I really don't think he wants to hurt you," I said. "I've been asking questions about Twila's death, and I think he's trying to intimidate me into stopping."

"Wait," he said. "Are you trying to solve the murder? Like Nancy Drew? Like *Sherlock*?" He seemed way more excited by the second one.

"No. I just thought that since I know the moms who were at the trade show, that I could ask questions to, you know, help the police."

"That's cool," he said. "Because *you* know you didn't do it, so you could help find out who did."

"Exactly," I said. "I didn't know it would lead to… this."

"No biggie." He pushed the hair out of his eyes. "Hey, my mom's a badass." I laughed.

* * * *

We got good news and bad news about my dad. His lungs were recovering nicely but he had to stay in the hospital one more night. Several of his friends were in and out during the afternoon, and Lani stopped by with Pico's dinner for us, even sneaking my dad his favorite chicken chimichangas.

Even though my dad was itching to get home, part of him seemed to be enjoying the attention. When he and Elliot were engrossed in a guitar lesson, I slipped out and Lani followed. I'd already texted her about the incident at Elliott's camp and knew she wanted to talk about it. We walked out of listening range.

"I know you're thinking it was a mistake to look into Twila's murder." She had her *Lani on a mission* expression. "But you're wrong. You couldn't have known this guy would do this."

I didn't think it was a mistake, but I couldn't help feeling a bit of panic as the night approached. "I know all that. But my kid might be in danger. And my dad is in the hospital. I can't be two places at once."

"The only reason for that dude to be trying to scare you would be that you're getting closer," she said. "You can't give up now."

"I'm not giving up." Maybe I had too much of my dad's stubbornness in me.

"Good. Elliott can stay with us tonight. We have a state-of-the-art security system. You know we'll guard him with our lives," she said, and from her it didn't sound overly dramatic. "You stay with your dad. It's just one more night."

I bit my lip, not wanting to let my son out of my sight.

"We'll even pick up Trouble," she said. "You, your dad, and Elliott—and Trouble—will be together at home tomorrow night, safe and sound."

Something told me it wouldn't be that easy.

* * * *

I spent the first few hours at the hospital clicking away on my laptop while my dad slept, updating my accounts and generating labels that I'd print out at home for orders that had come in on the website. Of course, the more time-consuming part was preparing the food for shipment, but at least I was being productive.

Lani sent me detailed texts about Elliott's status. *He ate 4 pieces of lasagna and 3 large chunks of Italian bread. He just pretended to eat the salad.*

Then, *What the heck is he reading? His book has zombie entrails on the front!*

He's asleep and Trouble is watching over him.

Lani also sent me her updated notes on the suspects. I filled in anything she was missing and emailed it back.

She replied right away. *I think you need a lice treatment*, with several bug emojis.

Oh man. She wanted me to check out the Lice Club Lady. That just creeped me out. *I think YOU need a lice treatment*, I texted back.

I can do it! she replied. *It's just a nice oil hair treatment, and my split ends could use it!*

Unfortunately, my sense of responsibility raised its ugly head and I told her, *It's okay. I'll handle it*, and reassured her *Are you sure?* messages.

Finally, I typed *Get some rest!* and fell asleep myself.

* * * *

I slept through at least two nighttime visits from nurses checking my dad's vitals and felt so much better the next morning. Unfortunately, my dad's temperature was up and even though he felt much better, the doctor handling the morning rounds recommended keeping him one more day.

My dad was very disappointed. "You don't need to stay," he told me. "I feel better now than I have in weeks. And Annie will be here soon. Go do your business stuff and whatever else you're working on that you're trying to keep a secret from me." Did he have parent ESP going on?

"And don't skip that farmers' market," he added. "You need to show your advisor guy and Twomey's that you got what it takes."

After only a little more insisting by my dad, I headed out, hoping to catch Elliott before he left for camp. Too bad he texted that he and Lani had dropped Trouble off at home and were on their way a little early to his camp.

Trouble was delighted to see me. She meowed loudly, demanding to know where I'd been, where my dad was, and why Elliott made her sleep somewhere else.

I sat at the kitchen table, watching her trying to grumble and eat at the same time. I was behind on my new product development. Trouble hadn't taste-tested any new recipes since her rejection of the curry chicken.

Someone rang my doorbell and then knocked on the door, loudly. Oh my God. What if it was Tall Bald Man? Was he crazy enough to come here after the police almost got him yesterday?

I grabbed my phone and called Norma, hiding so whoever was there couldn't see me. "Norma," I whispered when she answered. "Someone is pounding on my door."

"Don't open it," she said firmly. "I'm on my way." She hung up.

"What?" I whispered again. How could she hang up?

I couldn't help it. I peeked my head around the corner and looked right into the eyes of Detective Little, who stood at the window just waiting for me.

I pulled my head back, too late.

"Open the damn door," he said.

I stayed where I was.

"Open the door or I'll break it down," he said.

I had an image of him knocking it right off its hinges like Hagrid did in the first Harry Potter movie, but Norma had said not to open it. He pounded on the door again, so hard the wall shook, and I gave in and opened the door.

"What do you want?" I demanded, amazed that my voice didn't quake.

"I'm here to ask you some questions, or you can come down to the station." He tried to keep his voice matter of fact, but he was enjoying himself.

"Why?" I asked, my insides beginning to quiver in the face of his nastiness. "I was cleared. You know I didn't kill Twila."

"Yeah, well, we got ourselves a whole 'nother murder," he said, satisfaction oozing through his voice. "And this one has your name all over it."

Another murder? A feeling of dread stunned me. "What the hell are you talking about?"

"That's what we have to discuss," he said, grabbing my arm. "Come with me."

I wrenched my arm away and backed into the house. "Come back with a warrant. Or with Norma. Cause I'm not going anywhere with you."

In what seemed like a split second, he had slammed me to the floor, put his knee in my back, and twisted my hands behind me. I screamed, and Trouble came flying out from the kitchen with a snarl that sounded as loud as a leopard. She leapt onto Little's head and he was forced to let go of my arm halfway through handcuffing me.

Then things started happening in slow motion. I heard Elliott yell, "Mom!" at the same time Lani screeched, "Get off her!" Both reached Little at the same time, pushing him off me while he was trying to unfasten Trouble from his head.

Little tumbled and Trouble landed easily, turning to attack again. I scrambled backwards and got to my feet. Then Little grabbed his gun and stood up in one smooth move, pointing it right at us.

"Just everybody calm down," I yelled and then repeated it more calmly, my voice shaking. I'd never been more terrified in my life.

Little's gun filled my vision, seeming as big as a missile launcher. I spread out my arms, the handcuff dangling from one of them, and slowly took a few steps so that Elliott and Lani were behind me. "You really don't want to do that. We are three unarmed civilians."

His eyes were steaming mad and blood oozed from a scratch at the top of his forehead. "You're all under arrest for assaulting a police officer," he yelled.

"Detective Little," Norma spoke firmly from the doorway.

I used my peripheral vision to see her standing with Detective Ragnor, who had his hand on his gun. Lani, Elliott, and I didn't move a muscle.

"Holster your weapon," Norma said. "Now," she added at a much lower octave when he didn't respond immediately.

I held my breath until he reluctantly followed her order. Then Ragnor grabbed him by the arm to drag him outside. "What the hell is wrong with you?" he asked Little.

"You all okay?" Norma asked.

I pulled Elliott into my arms and hugged him tight, crying.

Lani hugged him as well, making a little Elliott sandwich, and then she pulled herself up straight and said, "I'd like to file a complaint. Police brutality."

Norma nodded. "I understand," she said. "But you might want to hold off a bit." She looked at Elliott and then asked me, "Can I speak to you in the kitchen?"

I nodded, letting Lani take over the whole hugging tight thing, and followed her, wiping my tears away with shaking hands.

"We found the man who threatened you," she said, completely professional. Then she ruined the whole thing by handing me a tissue.

I blew my nose. "Really? Did he tell you why he was harassing us?"

"No," she said slowly. "He didn't say much at all."

"Why not?" I asked.

"He's dead."

Chapter 16

I couldn't take anymore. I collapsed into a chair and put my head down on the table. "Where?" I asked. "When?" My mind was spinning. "Is that what Little was talking about?" With more time, I was sure to come up with more questions.

"He was found shot to death in the Sunnyside Lake Park. The station got an anonymous phone call implicating you. That was followed up by an email with a photo attached." She was telling me just the facts, but I could tell she was holding something back.

"Okay," I said slowly. "Can I see the picture?"

She pulled it up on her phone. It was a photo of me facing him down outside the ice cream shop. I enlarged the part that showed me. My hands were in fists and I look enraged, certainly mad enough to kill. Only the back of his head was shown.

"The detective jumped to conclusions," she said.

"How about coming to a different conclusion about why someone was even taking this photo?" I asked.

She didn't answer.

"This just shows the back of his head," I said. "How did he know it was the same guy?"

"There's a distinctive indentation on the back of his head," she said.

I shuddered. "What's his name?" I asked.

"We're not sure yet," she said. "He was stripped of ID and his fingerprints aren't in the system. A black SUV was seen speeding away during the night but the body wasn't found until a hiker stumbled across it this morning. The first officer on the scene recognized him from your sketch. And then the phone call and email came in."

I shook my head, my face still scrunched against the table. "This makes no sense at all."

"I need to ask," Norma said, "where were you last night between the hours of midnight and two am?"

"Luckily for me, I guess, I was in the hospital with my dad," I said. "I'm sure there's about a zillion security cameras there that can verify it. And the nursing staff."

"That's good," Norma said. "Don't worry. I'll handle Little."

"I hope so," I said. "He's losing his freakin' mind."

She shrugged. "It's complicated." She filled me in on the phone call Little had mentioned in his testosterone-filled scene outside our house when he'd backed down from Norma and Detective Ragnor. On the night of Twila's someone had called the station and left an anonymous message that they'd seen me hiding something in the garbage can. That, combined with my dad and me finding the body, led to Norma being able to get a search warrant so quickly. Even though her gut told her we didn't kill Twila, she had to follow procedure.

But Little had the opposite reaction. His gut told him we were involved and he just couldn't let go. So when the second anonymous call came in, he thought he had me.

Norma tried to explain. "Sometimes police decide that their intuition is more important than the evidence. They could believe someone is guilty when all the evidence is pointing the other way."

"Are they usually macho jerks?" I asked.

She smiled, but didn't agree out loud. "Sometimes it works the other way. He, or she, can believe someone is innocent when they're not."

"What's going to happen to Little?" I asked.

"He'll be disciplined," she said. "Severely."

"That doesn't help Elliott."

She nodded her head toward my son who was acting out what happened for Ragnor, pretending to be Little and then switching to playing Lani, me, and Trouble. "He looks like he's bouncing back."

* * * *

Sunnyside didn't have a lot of murders, so two in such a short period of time was big news.

Elliott insisted on going to camp, thinking that late was better than never, and Lani insisted on dropping him off. The only reason they'd been at home in time to see Little attack me was because Elliott had forgotten his voice recorder that helped him learn his lines. Since they had extra time, they'd returned to get it.

Norma had told Elliott not to talk about what happened that morning to anyone. I didn't know how he could keep it a secret.

Some part of me was relieved that Tall Bald Man wasn't around to scare us, but that made me feel terrible. Even if he was a big bully, he was a real person, and he was dead.

* * * *

I thought I knew what tired felt like, but the emotional toll of the encounter with Little on top of the last couple of nights in the hospital with my dad had me tumbling into bed in bright daylight and asleep as soon as I pulled up the covers.

I'd set my alarm for one hour but woke up two hours later with no memory of turning the alarm off. My phone had two text messages from Annie letting me know that she was hanging with my dad and that he seemed fine, despite his fever.

Norma had returned our phones and computers. They were all charged and I wondered if they'd been able to read any messages we'd sent and received. I picked up my dad's phone and saw a message from Gypsy Sue, something about visiting him in the hospital.

What? Sue from the farmers' markets knew my dad?

I could only see the first line of the last couple of messages on the screen, so I decided to see if I could break my dad's password. It was pretty easy—Elliott's birthday. It didn't occur to me until it worked that maybe I shouldn't be invading my dad's privacy.

I ignored everything else but the history of messages with Sue. She had arranged to visit him when I wasn't there. What was that about? I scrolled through. The messages showed that they were friends. The messages on the phone went back over a year, but it was clear they knew each other far longer.

I thought back to how I'd met Sue when she was a new volunteer with the nonprofit for teen moms. I always thought it was a lucky coincidence that we'd been matched up. Did she know my dad back then?

After downing a second cup of coffee, I couldn't stand it any longer. I called her using my dad's phone.

"Hey, big guy," she said.

I was silent a moment. "This is Colbie."

"Oh." I could imagine her covering the phone and swearing.

"You want to tell me anything?" I asked.

She didn't answer for a minute. "You should talk to your dad."

"Really? While he's in the hospital?" I asked. "Have you been spying on me all these years?"

"Colbie," she said. "You know me better than that." She paused. "Your dad wanted to make sure you were safe and cared for. And you have been."

I shook my head, trying to make sense of it. "He asked you to do it?"

"Yes."

"Why?" I asked.

"You don't need to be psychic to know the answer to that," she said. "He loves you."

I shook my head in bewilderment, my anger dying away. "Can you start at the beginning?"

She didn't say anything for long time. "I think that's a conversation you need to have with your dad, when he's feeling better."

I didn't say anthing.

"Just know that he was always there for you."

* * * *

Did my dad put Sue in my life? I remembered all the times Sue had magically fixed problems for us. Finding me the job at the apartment complex when I aged out of the single mothers program. Encouraging me to start my own business. Had that really been my dad pulling the strings in order to help me out?

I swallowed to get rid of the lump of regret in my throat, and changed gears to save my sanity. When my dad was home, we'd talk. I packaged up my back-logged orders and dropped them off to be shipped, which was really the rock bottom of being a responsible business owner. I should be doing so much more, especially with the Twomey's decision hanging over my head.

A responsible business owner certainly shouldn't be calling the number on the Lice Club Lady card and leaving a message asking for an emergency appointment for lunch time. But then, most responsible business owners didn't have their family threatened.

I had to admit to myself that I was being a bit stubborn. Okay, maybe more than a bit. No one believed I'd killed Twila. Well, maybe some piece of Little's tiny brain still thought there was a chance. But I couldn't let it go. No matter how much I argued with myself that Norma was a thorough and competent detective, here I was, taking steps to find out more about someone who probably wasn't a suspect, but might know something that would lead to the suspect. And a big part of me believed that we wouldn't be safe until the killer was found.

I received a call back a few minutes later from a young woman asking if a noon lice check appointment worked for me. Her voice wasn't familiar at all—she wasn't an SPM member.

She gave me weird instructions. "You'll drive to Rushdall Park where you'll park and walk across the lawn to the wooden fence. Turn left and follow the fence until you come to a gate on your right. I'll open it right before your appointment and meet you there."

"Okay," I said, drawing it out. "This is like spy stuff. What's the big deal?"

"We go the extra mile to guarantee our customers' privacy," she said in a reassuring tone. "I'll see you at twelve."

A responsible business owner certainly wouldn't find herself at the Rushdall Park a little before noon, walking past the nearly empty playground that even the most dedicated parent wouldn't brave in this heat, and standing at the gate as it opened a few minutes before noon. And she wouldn't be following a young lady dressed in light blue scrubs through a private backyard lined with trees on both sides so there was no way for a neighbor to see in.

And yet, here I was. Walking through a rear entrance to someone's garage that had been renovated to look just like a regular hair salon. Except instead of assorted scissors and fancy brushes, the counter held a bunch of combs in disinfectant and a squeeze bottle.

"Whose property is this?" I asked.

"I actually don't know," she said. "My boss rents it." She turned the hair salon chair around. "Please take a seat."

She opened a cabinet and pulled out a large jug, and poured some of it in the squeeze bottle. The smell of lavender mixed with a woody scent filled the salon. I peeked inside and saw fabric covered boxes.

Was this Sharon's work? If so, maybe she knew who the Lice Club Lady was.

Then I remembered something Fawn said. That Sharon had done work for her other business.

"This salon is perfect," I said. "You wouldn't even know it was originally a garage. And it's so well organized."

"The owner had a professional do it." The technician applied the oil to my hair and combed it through, parting it to examine a section of my scalp. "So far, so good," she said. "No indication of any creatures."

"That's great." I continued to play along. "My head has been itching like crazy ever since I heard about the outbreak."

"This treatment is very soothing," she said. "Even if you don't have a problem, it'll make your scalp feel better." She continued combing and checking the comb after each stroke.

"Do you know who did the job here?" I asked. "My dad could use help with his garage."

"Something like Soldier Closet maybe?" she said. "I could ask the owner for you."

I was right! Sharon's closet business was Closet Commando. "That's okay. I'll Google that." I waited while she combed through another section of my hair. "So this is an interesting job to have," I said. "How did you get it?"

"Through a special program for foster kids," she said.

Foster youth? Fawn ran a nonprofit that found jobs for foster youth.

That nailed it. Fawn was the Lice Club Lady.

* * * *

I called Lani as soon as I hiked back through the park and made it to the car. "Do you know who the Lice Club Lady is?" I asked, as the air conditioner brought the temperature down to a bearable level.

"No," she answered. "Did you figure it out?"

"Yes," I said. "It's your good friend Fawn."

"Wow." She took a minute to think it through. "She really is *excellent* at keeping secrets. Maybe it's all that life coach training."

"Lani," I said. "I asked her straight out and she didn't answer me. Maybe she has something to hide."

"I can't imagine Fawn hurting anyone," Lani insisted and then relented. "But I guess you should ask her if she's hiding anything that would help."

"I'm going to see her now," I said. "Oh, shoot. The SPM moms will be there soon. Sharon's holding an open house to show off Fawn's garage." And I needed to talk to Fawn in private.

"Do you know when you say SPM moms, you're really saying Sunnyside Power Moms Moms?" Lani asked.

"I know," I said. "It's just easier."

"I'm going to call Piper and see if that brat knew this whole time and didn't tell me," Lani said.

"And I'm going to suck it up and talk to Fawn on the way to the Farmers' Market, even if I have to get her away from the other SPM *moms*. She has to answer my questions, whether she likes it or not." Stopping there was going to make me late for the market again. Two weeks in a row—the manager would be really unhappy with me now. But I'd deal with that later. And this way, I'd be able to pick up Elliott from camp and take him with me to help.

"You go girl," Lani cheered. "I've always wanted to say that."

I went home to pack up my car with everything I needed for the farmers' market, hustled Trouble into her cat carrier, and drove over to Fawn's. I had to park a few doors down, and since I couldn't leave the cat in the car, I dragged the carrier with me.

Lani had texted that Piper didn't know and didn't care who the Lice Club Lady was. She did good work and anything that helped prevent the spread of lice was welcomed.

I put down the cat to text back. *She's not worried about the secrecy aspect?*

Nope, Lani texted back. *People are bound to be embarrassed. If the treatments reduce the problem, it's all good with her.*

I could tell something was going on as soon as I walked up the driveway. Gina, Fawn, and Daria were all there, standing in the perfect garage and staring at me with baleful looks, while Sharon was demonstrating how efficient her garage closet designs were to a woman I didn't know.

"What's wrong?" I asked the three women.

Daria took the lead, keeping her voice quiet so Sharon's potential customer couldn't hear. "We all know what you're doing."

"What am I doing?" I asked.

Trouble growled in her carrier. *Let my human alone!* She didn't like this confrontation either.

Gina took a step forward. "We compared notes and realized that you are desperate to find someone else to blame for Twila's murder."

Daria lifted her chin. "And any of us will do."

"That is not true," I said. "The police have cleared me."

"Right," Gina said, her ponytail bobbing indignantly. "Then why are you still looking into it?"

"Because I want the truth," I said. "And so should all of you."

They didn't look convinced.

"Look," I said. "My son was threatened twice. And the man who threatened him is dead now too."

"What? That's who was in the news today?" Gina demanded.

"Yes. So I'll back off when people stop getting killed," I said, wondering how I got so tough.

Unfortunately, Sharon's sales target heard the last word and turned around. Sharon scowled and jerked her head toward the driveway. A clear *get out* signal.

Trouble went into full spitting attack mode, and the women took a step away from us.

"Fawn, I need to speak to you." I scowled at the others. "Alone."

They met each other's eyes, finding the mean girl inside of them. "I don't think you should," Daria told Fawn.

I shrugged and ran my hand through my hair. "Fine with me," I said. "I can just tell everyone what I learned today in my walk through Rushdall Park."

Her big doe eyes grew larger. "I'll be right back, ladies."

She followed me toward the street, and Trouble calmed down. We stopped by a group of three small palm trees beside her driveway and I turned to face away from the ladies who were watching us like hawks.

"I think that you learned something through your Lice Club Lady business that has to do with Twila." I was pushing her with nothing more than a hunch. "You need to tell me what that is."

"Are you threatening me?" she asked, belligerent.

Aha! She did know something. "Just tell me," I demanded.

"Or else what?"

"What do you think?" I *probably* wouldn't divulge her secret, but she didn't need to know that. "Someone came after my kid. If telling people you run an underground business will keep people away from him, you know I'll do it."

Her face grew only slightly less angry. "Fine. Mona gave lice to Twila's husband, Trent. You can imagine how that happened."

Shoot. Was she saying that Mona had an affair with him? I felt sick to my stomach, but forced myself to pull out my phone and bring up the photo I'd taken of the man going into Mona's house. "Is this Trent?" He didn't fit the description, but it was worth a shot.

She scoffed. "No. That's the husband of the PTA president." She looked closer. "Is that Mona's house? She's really playing with fire now. Does she want her kids to get the worst teachers the rest of their lives?"

That might be true. "So you think Mona was having an affair with Trent and now this guy?" I asked.

"Yes," she said. "Because of the lice. First Mona was here, and then Trent. And then Twila's kids. So he gave it to them, not the other way around."

"That's your evidence?" I asked.

"There have been plenty of rumors about her with other married men," she said flatly. "I ignored them before this."

"Did Twila know?"

"I have no idea," she said. "She never mentioned anything to me."

"What did Twila think about your business?" I asked. Maybe the secrecy was the unethical behavior she was upset about.

"She was the only one I confided in," Fawn said. "And she thought the secret club thing was brilliant marketing."

I paused, trying to make sense of this possible affair. "Okay, now that everyone knows what I'm doing, is there anything you or the others aren't telling me?"

"No," she said, but she looked troubled.

"Fawn," I said, tired of the BS. "I found out about your underground business. You may as well just tell me because I'm going to find out whatever it is."

She promptly burst into tears and I ended patting her arm. "It's okay," I said automatically as Trouble stared up at us. *What's her problem?*

"I—" She interrupted herself with a couple of sobs and then got herself under control. "I was the last one to leave."

"Okay," I said. "Do the police know that?"

She nodded. "I heard a noise outside when I left." She started crying again. "And I didn't stop to see what, or who, it was."

I stopped cold, understanding her guilt before she said it out loud. "Did you tell the police what you heard?"

She nodded, tearing up. "I didn't want the other moms to know. If I hadn't been in such a rush," she admitted in a wail. "Twila might still be alive."

Chapter 17

It took me a while to comfort Fawn, which gave me even less time to confront Mona before I picked up Elliott.

This time, she didn't answer the door in lingerie. "We meet again," she said in her sexy voice.

Maybe she always talked that way.

"I'm in a hurry and I need to know if you had an affair with Twila's husband," I said right out.

Trouble was licking her paw in her carrier and didn't even acknowledge Mona.

"Whatever gave you that idea?" she asked.

It was time to get tough. I held up the Lice Club Lady card, and her mouth made a little O of surprise.

"It seems like you were the center of an outbreak," I said. "And if you don't want me to put that on SDHelp, you better tell me everything."

"You wouldn't," she said.

When I simply raised my eyebrows, she huffed and said, "Fine." Then she looked up and down the block. "Just come inside so none of the neighbors see you. They hate me enough as it is."

I expected her home to look like a den of inequity, whatever that looked like, but it was completely modern, with off-white furniture and light oak accent pieces.

"First of all, let's get something straight. Despite what you may have heard, I don't have affairs with married men. And I'm not some kind of prostitute," she said. "My business is to help people enjoy healthy relations with their significant others. I sell massage oils and toys, not myself."

"What was Trent doing here?" I asked.

She gave a heavy sigh. "I'm also a registered masseuse, and I use that to teach men how to give their partners a sensual massage."

"On you?" I asked.

"No, you idiot," she insisted. "On these two." She opened a hall closet and two very realistic mannequins were staring out at me. One male. One female. Anatomically correct.

That took the wind out of my sails. "Did Twila know her husband was here?"

"I don't know," she said. "She certainly didn't say anything if she did. And of course, I would never tell."

"Why do you do this?" I couldn't help but ask.

"Since I started directing my marketing to men, I've quadrupled my sales," she said proudly. "I'm the number one salesperson in the southwest region. This sort of grew from that. Men need a lot more help than most people realize."

"Why were you wearing lingerie the last time I was here?" I asked. "When the PTA president's husband stopped by."

She stood up straight, offended. "He is separated from her and we are dating. Not that it's any of your business."

Oh man. This stuff was hard. And the separation was not going to save her kids from the PTA president's wrath. I forced myself to ask another question. "Was there any chance Trent was learning, um, that for someone else other than Twila?"

She shook her head. "Absolutely not. He was totally in love with her. He was devastated at the funeral."

I believed her. Another dead end.

* * * *

I had to put Twila and the new dead guy out of my head. Elliott and I grabbed burgers, fries, and shakes from In-n-Out, and ate on the way to the farmers' market. Sue waved from across the aisle but didn't stop over.

Elliott noticed. "Is she mad at you?" he asked, rubbing Trouble under the chin. She stretched out her neck with her eyes closed.

"Nah," I said. "Probably just busy." I turned away to deal with a customer and when I turned back, Sue was right in front of me, looking troubled.

"You good?" she asked.

In response, I gave her a long hug. "With you, yes." I wasn't sure about everything else.

* * * *

I let Elliott go into my dad's hospital room and hang out with him while I headed down to the cafeteria so I could call Lani. I told her all about my progress. "Hold on while I get my computer," she said.

I waited until she came back to finish. The room was mostly empty, with one table of nurses enjoying the chicken teriyaki special.

"You're really ramping it up now," she said.

Piper spoke in the background. "Is that Colbie? How is she?"

"She's fine," Lani told her. "You're fine, right?"

"Yeah." I tried to calm my uneasiness. "I just can't shake the feeling that I'm running out of time. Can we go over this list? We have to be missing something." I paid the cashier for the soda and headed back to my dad's room.

"You talked to just about everyone we put on," she said. "How did all of those moms seem today?"

"Defensive. Angry." Something jogged my memory. "You know what? After Norma cleared Bert, I never checked to see if his security code sounded the same as the one at the activity center."

"The one that sounds like Beethoven's' Fifth?" she asked. "Well you can't go tonight. That would be stupid."

"Yeah, you're right," I said. "I'll go first thing tomorrow."

"The other big thing you haven't followed up on is talking to Tod Walker," she said.

"Yeah," I said. "Norma told me to stay away from him."

"Ooh," Lani said. "That sounds interesting."

I smiled. "Maybe I can squeeze him in tomorrow, too."

Elliott came into the hall. "Hey, Mom. Did you know Grandpa saw the Northern Lights once? And he could hear them crackling."

"Gotta go," I told Lani. I hung up and joined him in my dad's room. "That's very cool."

* * * *

Since my dad was doing so much better, I slept at home that night and dropped Elliott off at camp before heading over to the hospital. I spent Fridays cooking for my original clients, but I was delighted to be bringing my dad home instead.

My dad looked better than he had in weeks when they wheeled him out to my waiting car and he got in. His face was pink and he'd lost that gaunt look that I'd almost become used to. He smiled the whole trip home, the smile stretching to a grin when we pulled in the driveway.

I looked at the house, realizing that in a few short weeks, it had become home for me again. Especially now that my dad was climbing the front steps.

"Welcome home," I said.

A package with a handwritten "Colbie" was waiting for me on the porch when we got there. I picked it up as my dad walked inside. He sat down in his chair with a sigh. "It's good to be home," he said.

"Coffee?" I asked.

"I'd love some," he said. "Thanks."

I made him a fresh pot and then ripped open the package.

It was the Merritt Finance binder I'd seen in Fawn's office. Maybe since I hadn't shared her Lice Club Lady secret she was willing to help me look into Bert's business. I paged through it. All of Fawn's personal information had been blacked out with a permanent marker. But there were still plenty of numbers in there.

I guess she was on my side. But what should I do with it?

Quincy! This was right up his alley. I called him and he answered on the first ring. "Good news?"

His voice was so excited that I almost felt bad for not knowing anything about the status of the Twomey's proposal. Although it had only been two days, two very long days, and they said it would take two weeks. "No, sorry. I wanted to see if you could help me with another issue." I explained about the binder.

"I'm out of town today," he said. "You can drop it off at the kitchen, and I'll take a look tomorrow."

"Thank you," I said.

"What do you think I'm going to find?" he asked.

"I don't know," I admitted. "Maybe it'll simply be a good investment opportunity." We said our good-byes and I delivered my dad's coffee.

"Thanks," he said. "But you don't need to take care of me." He pulled out his cell phone. "I feel so good that I'm going to call a few folks and see if they want to come over for lunch."

I must have looked alarmed because he laughed. "Don't worry. I'm ordering pizza."

"Save me some," I said. "Are you sure you're okay? If you really don't need me to be here, I can get some errands out of the way."

He waved his hand around. "Get outta here," he said, sounding more like he was from New York than Boston.

"Okay," I said. "Call if you need anything." I went up to my room to research Tod Walker, the man who had threatened Twila over a puzzle. Only one Todrick Walker lived in San Diego. I looked up what he'd written on Twila's website and he'd included his number for her to call him! Wow. I bet putting it on a public site resulted in a lot of junk calls.

I called Mr. Walker and he didn't answer, so I left a message explaining that I was a friend of Twila's and that I'd like to talk to him.

Then I got impatient and decided to see if he was home. I didn't tell my dad where I was going but I texted Lani. *Looked up Todrick Walker and there's only one in San Diego. I'm going to talk to him.*

Good luck! she texted back. *Stay safe!*

Todrick Walker, which was a fun name to say, lived in downtown San Diego, not very far from the apartment building I used to manage.

Lani called. "Maybe you shouldn't be going alone."

"It's in my old 'hood," I said. "And I doubt that someone so obsessed with puzzles is dangerous."

His building was so much like my old apartment building—the same cracked pavement in front, the cement porch with graffiti that I'd regularly scrubbed off, the labeled doorbells behind yellowing plastic. Before living in suburbia, I wouldn't have noticed the smells emanating from the overflowing garbage cans or the grimy steps.

I had a moment's hesitation before heading up the stairs.

I pressed the doorbell marked Walker in 3B. It looked like it had been there for a while, with typed letters. All the others had handwritten names.

It took a long time for him to answer. "Yes?"

"Hi, Mr. Walker," I said using my most chipper voice. "My name is Colbie. I'm a friend of Twila Jenkins, and I was wondering if we could talk."

I waited. No answer. I heard a click, which gave me the impression he was still there, listening.

"Mr. Walker?" I asked.

"Why?" he asked.

"I'm trying to find out what happened to her," I said, wondering if that was the wrong thing to say.

"Which friend are you?" he asked through the intercom.

"Excuse me?"

"How do you know her?"

This was just about the weirdest conversation I'd had in a while. "Um, I'm one of the moms in her group. I sell cat food."

He didn't answer.

"Look, would you like to come out and have a cup of coffee with me?" I asked.

Nothing.

"Or maybe another time?"

The intercom clicked, and all he said was, "No."

Really? Was he afraid of me? I looked at my phone, and decided I had time to wait for one of his neighbors to come along. He'd have to talk to me if I yelled from outside his apartment. Then an Amazon Fresh truck pulled up and a young woman slid open the side door. She pulled out a bunch of green cooler bags and ran up the stairs. I moved out her way and she gave the 3B button three short buzzes.

"You know Tod?" I asked. "He won't let me in."

She gave me the once over and seemed to decide that I was harmless. "He doesn't let anyone in." A buzzer sounded and she pulled open the door. "Sorry I can't help. I could lose my job."

"No problem," I said, fuming a bit. Luckily a young man with a skateboard, and a key, skidded to a halt in front of the building, flipped the skateboard under his arm, and unlocked the door. I followed him in and took the stairs at a half run. The delivery woman was still coming down the hall from the elevator.

She set the bags down in front of 3B, knocked three times, waved toward the ceiling, and turned around.

I looked up and saw a security camera. "Have you met him?" I asked her.

"Nope," she said cheerfully and jogged down the stairs.

I waved at the camera like she had and leaned against the opposite wall to wait. I heard the floor creak near the door. "Don't you want your food?" I asked.

"Go away." There was genuine fear in his voice.

Shoot. I was being a big ol' bully. Like Tall Bald Man.

"I'm really sorry. I'm not trying to scare you. I'm just trying to figure out what happened to my friend."

I heard shuffling near the door and tried another tactic. "Can you tell me one thing? Why did you complain about Twila's puzzles?"

"They were wrong," Tod said. "There was more than one answer. There has to be one right answer."

"What did she say when you complained?"

"She apologized and fixed it," he said. "I helped her solve puzzles."

"Did you ever meet her?" I asked.

"No." His voice became more agitated. "I need my food."

"I'm sorry to bother you," I said. "I'll go."

"Okay."

"Okay." I put my card on the linoleum floor near his food. "Can you contact me if you think of anything that might help me figure things out?"

"Like a puzzle?"

"Yes," I said. "Like a puzzle."

He seemed to consider it before answering. "Maybe."

I headed down the stairs, realizing why Norma had wanted me to stay away from him. He was a shut-in of some kind, perhaps even agoraphobic.

Maybe he was helping Norma somehow. Tod really liked puzzles. Could he be helping Norma solve the puzzle of Twila's murder?

He said he solved puzzles for Twila. Did he solve the wrong puzzle?

Chapter 18

Soon I was on the road back to Sunnyside. For the first time I appreciated just how pretty it was. No smelly garbage. No graffiti. People kept up their houses and yards, even when their plants were drooping in the summer heat.

Was I ready to become a small-town girl? I wasn't sure. Was Elliott? At some point, we'd have to decide.

But in the meantime, I had one more errand to do.

I'd set my GPS to Bert's office. It was on the outskirts of Sunnyside, set in a one-story building filled with small offices, including a business offering meeting rooms for rent. I tried the glass door to Suite 103, with Merritt Financial painted on it, but it was locked.

I knocked and nothing happened. I put my hand up to shield my eyes and looked through the tinted glass. All I saw were a few empty desks with computers sitting on them. Someone had placed neat stacks of paper beside them, but it didn't look real. It looked more like a movie set of an office than an office where real people worked.

It was close to eleven, certainly too early for lunch, even for a Friday. What was going on?

The security panel was right there. I tried a few buttons. It didn't sound anything like musical notes at all, just faint clicks.

Had Bert really been at the activity center that night?

I was about to take off when I saw someone drive in. I waited for a woman about my age to get out and walk toward Suite 104, which looked like a tech company. "Do you know when Merritt Financial opens?" I asked.

She shook her head. "I haven't worked here long, but I've never seen them actually open."

What was going on?

* * * *

I didn't have time to figure it out. Fridays were half days at Elliott's camp, so I picked him up and we went out to lunch to give my dad some time with his friends. I noticed that he had a hole in his sneakers and two hours later, we'd picked up new shoes and a few theater T-shirts.

Elliott was in an unusually subdued mood. I'd decided not to ask about him contacting his father; as each day went on without a response, it would only hurt to have me remind him. But I couldn't help but wonder how he felt about it.

"Everything okay?" I asked yet again and he nodded.

"I hope Grandpa feels good enough to see the performance next week," he said.

"Me too," I said, not wanting to give him any guarantees. "He's much better today."

We drove into the driveway in time to see Annie come out from the house. "Colbie! I'm so glad you're here," she said, giving Elliott a brief hug. "I was having too good a time with your dad and his friends and I totally forgot about my big box delivery from Joss. Can you guys pick it up for me? I'd really appreciate it."

I remembered that Joss sold organic produce in a subscription service. "You mean the organic veggies?" I asked.

"Yes," she said. "His newsletter says he's including strawberries and I don't want them to go to waste."

"Sure," Elliott said, the prospect of seeing the chicks brightening his face. "I'll get it."

"I'll come too," I said.

"Mom," he said. "The guy who was bothering me is dead. I can go alone."

I answered mildly, "I haven't seen the chicks in a while."

Annie must have let Joss know we were coming because he was waiting on the porch. "I could've brought it down."

"It's no bother," I said. "Elliott wanted to see the chicks."

He didn't respond to my smile. "Go ahead, Elliott," he said. "I need to talk to your mother."

We both waited for him to walk through the pen into the chicken coop. "What's up?"

"I'm sorry," he said, not looking at me. "I can't have you, either of you, coming over here."

"Okay," I said slowly. "You want to tell me why?"

He pushed his hand through his hair, his frustration making me feel marginally better. "My ex-wife called threatening to tell the judge that my home is not safe for Kai since you and Elliott…"

"You mean, because known criminals like me and my twelve-year-old son stop by once in a while to see your chicks?" I couldn't keep the anger out of my voice. "Is she watching you or something?"

He shook his head. "I mentioned something to Kai about you guys. I shouldn't have. My ex takes every advantage that she can." He didn't seem to like it any better than I did.

"Well, great," I said. "That'll really make Elliott's day. After all the crap he's had to go through."

"I know," he said. "I'm sorry. But Kai comes first."

"Wonderful," I said, getting louder. "Perhaps you could've thought of that before you messed with my son's head. Did he tell you he contacted his biological father? And now he's going to have to face the fact that not everyone wants to be a parent like you. And what about me?" I was really losing control. "I've been both of his parents his whole life and now I have to worry that his dad, who has never contacted me in thirteen years, may want to swoop in here and take him away from me. So, thanks. Thanks a lot for all of that."

Joss's face looked stunned. Then his eyes moved to something behind me.

I whirled around. Elliott was standing there. Heartbreak was all over his face. "You don't have to worry, Mom," he said. "He messaged me back."

I took a step toward him, my heart breaking along with him.

"My 'dad' doesn't want me. He doesn't want anything to do with me." Tears started spilling from his eyes.

I clumsily opened the gate. "It's okay," I murmured.

He stared at me like I was crazy. "But that's just fine with you, right? You get to keep me all to yourself."

I gasped.

He started crying in earnest, and pushed right by me, angry, embarrassed, and grief-stricken.

I stared after him, stunned. "I don't think I could have messed that up any worse," I said to Joss.

* * * *

I barely pulled myself together to greet my dad's friends before heading up to my room. I dug around in the closet until I found one of the few boxes I hadn't put in storage when we moved in. It was labeled "Hoodies." I'd never been the kind of mom who made scrap books, but I had kept every hoodie of Elliott's that represented a stage of his life. There was one from his last play, *Joseph and Amazing Technicolor Dreamcoat*, the jacket from fifth grade when he'd decided to try the local swim team, and the one from *Lion King*, the first Broadway San Diego show I'd taken him to when he was six. I'd watched him notice how young the star was, and right at that moment, he'd fallen in love with the idea that kids could do theater.

I could create a book with this box. *Elliott's Life in Hoodies.* All the way back to the first one when he was a newborn. Impossibly small, it had "Tough Guy" printed on it.

I looked up to see Elliott in the doorway. He gave me a sad smile. "You still have all those?" He walked in and picked up one that said "Future President" over an American flag. "You can probably toss that one," he said.

"I don't know," I said. "From what I hear, politics is a heck of a lot like theater."

He sat down on the bed and at the same time, we both said, "I'm sorry."

I moved some jackets out of the way to sit beside him. "Let me go first." I gathered my thoughts. "My feelings about you contacting your dad were selfish, and that wasn't fair to you."

He shrugged one thin shoulder. "Mine were selfish too."

"You want to talk about it?" I asked. "Your father, I mean."

He got a faraway look in his eye. "I guess I wanted the Hollywood ending, you know? But he's just a big—." He cut himself off, probably not wanting to use that kind of language in front of me.

"What did his message say?" I asked, tentative.

"Just that he has no interest in having a relationship with me." His voice was more resigned than sad.

"That's it?" How could someone be that callous? I thought of the kid who held my hand in the university library and wanted to surf all the time. He must have changed.

I threw my arm around his shoulder. "You know it's his loss, right?"

"Oh yeah." He smiled. "Cause I'm awesome."

* * * *

Lani and Piper came over to celebrate my dad's return to health, bringing Chinese food and cheap champagne. I refused to talk about anything having to do with Twila, or murder, or anything not entirely positive. Elliott entertained us with bits of his musical, and backstage stories; some were from other musicals that he'd never told me before.

The cheap champagne made itself felt the next morning, and it took me longer than usual to get out of bed and get ready for the Little Italy Farmers' Market. Even Trouble seemed a little cranky and refused to wear her hat. Normally Saturdays were busy, but San Diego's "June Gloom" had started and the sky varied between a heavy marine layer and drizzle. Only my most devoted customers showed up. When some heavier rain started that was not in the forecast, I joined the other businesses who were packing up to go.

Sue stopped by to cuddle Trouble, and we both limited our conversation to small talk. I'd had just about enough drama lately. With my dad on the path to being healthy again, life should be going back to normal.

As I was loading the final box in the car, I got a text from Elliott. *Grandpa is going to the pub.*

I texted back *Are you going too?* I knew my dad was feeling better, but overdoing it at the pub is what put his health over the edge just a few days ago.

Elliott texted back *Just got Rot and Ruin eBook from library. Can I stay home and read it?*

I texted Annie to see if she could go with my dad—she replied that my dad had already invited her and she was delighted to—before letting Elliott off the hook.

Trouble meowed from her carrier. *He deserves a break.*

Sunnyside lived up to its name—I hit clear skies as soon as I crested the hill in Mission Trails Park but the day was still cool. I decided to stop at the grocery store and pick up everything to make my dad's favorite meal—broiled lamp chops with mashed potatoes and corn on the cob.

Trouble meowed, agreeing. *If one of those chops is for me, I'll wait quietly in the car.*

Then Quincy called when I pulled into a parking spot. I answered, letting the car run so the Bluetooth wouldn't be cut off. "Hi, Quincy."

He didn't bother with a greeting. "Where did that prospectus come from?" he asked.

"A friend has her money in that fund," I said. "Why?"

"Well, tell her to get it out immediately," he said. "It's bogus."

"Wait. What?" I asked even though some part of me thought, "*I knew it.*"

Trouble meowed at me from her carrier. *I knew it too.*

"I ran the numbers, and even had a colleague take an independent look at them," he said. "There's no way they match what's happened in the market. It can't possibly be getting the kind of return the documents are claiming."

"So what is he doing?" I asked, feeling breathless.

"It's most likely some kind of pyramid scheme," he said. "If you like, I can report it to the Sheriff's Financial Crimes Division."

Holy cow. "Um, yeah. I guess you better," I said.

An older woman walked by carrying empty grocery bags and gave me a funny look. Shoot. Could she hear what we were saying?

"I will," he said. "But call your friend before all the assets are frozen. And don't tell anyone I said that."

I was about to call Fawn, but then I had a terrible thought. Sharon also pushed this fund to all of us. Was Sharon the SPM member Twila was concerned about? Had Twila done what I did and asked someone else to look into it? My mind skittered away from what that might mean.

Todrick Walker. He said he solved puzzles for Twila. Had he solved this one? I searched my phone for all the times I'd tried to call him, and dialed it. He didn't answer so I left a message. "Hi, Tod. This is Twila's friend Colbie. Did you solve a financial puzzle for Twila? Can you call me back immediately? It's important."

I sat there, thinking through all the possibilities, willing Tod to call me back.

Nothing.

I texted him the same question, hoping that responding by text would be easier for him.

"..." appeared on my screen and I held my breath.

He texted. *Yes.*

Did you call her that night? I typed. I just couldn't type *the night she was killed.*

He texted back. *Yes*, with a sad-faced emoji. And then he typed a bunch of sad-faced emojis.

I'm so sorry, I texted. *Can I stop by tomorrow?* Maybe he could give me more info in person.

He texted. *Yes.*

I rested my head on the steering wheel for a moment. Had Twila confronted Sharon about the bogus fund? And had Sharon killed her for it? I pulled out of the parking spot.

Trouble meowed. *But what about my lamb chop?*

"It'll just have to wait." I used the stop light to dial Norma's number to tell her what I'd learned.

* * * *

As soon as I got home, I let Trouble out of her carrier and yelled upstairs. "Elliott! Come on down."

No answer.

I ran up the stairs. He wasn't there. Oh no, did he go visit the chicks? That was not going to make Joss happy. And going alone? I dialed Elliott and heard the phone ring from under his pillow. *He didn't take his phone with him? He knew that was our number one rule.*

I ran down the stairs and yanked open the front door before rushing down the street. My nervousness grew with each step. If he wasn't with the chicks, where could he be?

I let myself into the pen and opened the door to the coop, and heard him cooing to the chicks. I suddenly felt I could breathe.

"What are you doing?" I demanded.

The chirping chicks grew silent.

"Shush," he said. "You scared them. And me." He looked at my face. "What's wrong?"

"You came here when you weren't supposed to and you left your phone at home," I said, not knowing where to start about Sharon. "You're still not supposed to go anywhere alone." I hadn't told him that Joss didn't want us here.

"Sorry." He didn't mean it. "I brought Charlie home. And geez, I'm like, a block from the house." He lifted a chick to his face and it started pecking at the hair falling in his eyes. "I didn't think you'd be home yet."

"I left the farmers' market early," I said. "Come on. I need to make some calls."

"Okay," he said in a long suffering tone and placed the chick gently on the table.

I opened the door to the incubator room and saw that the outside door was closed.

"That's weird," Elliott said, going over to it immediately. "Joss only closes that at night. To keep out the coyotes and foxes." He pushed on it and it didn't move. "Shoot."

"Joss?" he called out.

I joined him. "Joss!"

Then I heard a voice.

"Joss isn't here."

I recognized that voice. It was Sharon.

Chapter 19

"Sharon?" I called out. "What's going on?" I could hear her footsteps walking away.

I pulled out my phone, dialed 911, and handed it to a scared looking Elliott. Then I pushed him toward the incubator room.

"Hello?" he said quietly into the phone and closed the door.

I called out Sharon's name a few times, hoping to block her ability to hear Elliott, and then I heard her come back. The smell of gasoline crept through the rough door. "Come on, Sharon, this joke isn't funny. Elliott's in here with me and he's scared."

"Then you should've kept your mouth shut," she said, "and he'd be safe and sound."

"What are you talking about?" I asked.

"I heard you at the grocery store," she said. "Right through the car."

"What do you mean?" I acted dumb.

She didn't fall for it. "You just couldn't leave well enough alone. You had to keep digging. You have only yourself to blame."

"For what?" I asked, my heart beating fast. "I found out your husband's fund isn't handled well. That's not the end of the world."

"You think I'm stupid?" she asked. "I was smart enough to shut up Twila and point the cops in your direction."

"You put that towel in my garbage can?" I had to keep her talking until the police got here. "But why?"

"I just wanted to get back to normal," she said. "But you wouldn't stop."

"Okay," I said. "I get it. I should've let it go. But why are you doing this?"

I heard liquid splash and the smell of gasoline became overwhelming. I panicked. "What are you doing?" I shoved the door back and forth, but whatever she'd done had wedged it shut. A small piece of wood splintered off into my hand.

"Because of you, Bert and I have to leave, and now I have to do this to keep the police busy until we can get across the border to Mexico." Her voice got louder. "Because of you, Bert is at the bank right now, getting all of the money out." She pounded on the door, shouting, "Because of you, I won't be able to see my babies, and my grandbabies ever again!"

"I'm so sorry," I yelled back, crying. "I didn't realize where this would lead. I was trying to help."

Without another word, she lit the gas on fire, and a whoosh of flames lit up the small room from the outside.

"Elliott!" I yelled and joined him in the incubator room. He was still on the phone with the police and his expression grew even more alarmed. "Tell them there's a fire!"

I saw a small hole in the corner and started chopping at the edges of the wood with my chunk of wood, trying to make the hole large enough to escape. Elliott ditched the phone and tried to ram the back door of the incubator room with his shoulder. It was also wedged tightly shut, and he gave up and joined me, digging at the hard ground with his bare hands. He stopped, and I yelled, "No, keep digging!"

He ignored me and tore off his shirt over his head, piling a bunch of chicks into it and returning to the corner. Smoke was coming in under the door from the coop, and he started shoving the chicks through the hole we'd made to the outside, in between my wild swings to break through the boards.

He went back for more chicks twice, filling his shirt while he coughed, and then joining me on the floor to let the chicks escape.

"Stay low!" I yelled, while tears streamed down my face. Smoke filled the small room, and I gasped for air as it felt like my lungs were seizing. The heat was overwhelming.

"I hear sirens," Elliott said through coughs, and we huddled together against the back door while flames licked up the inside wall just a few feet away.

Suddenly, the door behind us opened and we fell out at the feet of Lani and Horace, who both looked as scared as we felt. Lani grabbed Elliott and Horace pulled me up, half dragging us as we stumbled away to a safe distance where I collapsed.

"Mom?" I heard from a distance. I could've sworn I saw Trouble peering down at me right before I passed out.

Chapter 20

I woke up in the emergency room, with Elliott sitting up in the next bed and my dad in a chair between us. "She's awake," he said, relief clear in his voice.

The acrid smell of smoke stuck to me. Both Elliott and I had oxygen masks on. I sat up in the hospital bed, feeling dizzy and confused. The sounds of hospital machines beeping came from the closed white curtains around us.

"You're okay," my dad said. "And so is our boy. You just stay calm."

I tried to talk but just coughed.

"Mom," Elliott said, his voice hoarse. "I'm okay."

"You both be quiet, you hear?" My dad patted my arm. "And I'll tell you all I know."

I nodded, that small movement causing my head to pound.

"You and Elliott have smoke inhalation and the doctor says you shouldn't talk much," he said. "Elliott's doing better than you, but both of you have irritated throats and lungs. And your hands are a mess"

"Sharon?" I asked in hoarse whisper, starting another bout of coughing.

"You already know most of it. Norma said that you called her and told her about Sharon and Bert's pyramid scheme. She also said you suggested that maybe Twila confronted Sharon the night of the trade show and that Sharon killed Twila." He shook his head as if he couldn't believe people could do such a thing. "Sharon overheard you talking to Quincy at the grocery store and followed you home. She said she wanted to distract the police so they could get out of town." He paused, the emotion clearly taking a toll, and then he cleared his throat. "She saw you go down to the farm and locked you in that chicken coop. She claims she didn't know Elliott was in there with you, but he said she's lying."

I nodded.

"Lani heard through the grapevine that the police arrested Bert at the bank, and she came by to tell you the good news. You didn't answer the door and Trouble was having a fit inside. She opened the door and your cat shot like an arrow down to the farm. Lani figured out right away that she was playing Lassie and ran after her. Horace came out and told her you guys were in there. Then she saw the fire and realized what Trouble was trying to tell her."

"Trouble saved us," Elliott said in a rough whisper. "And Lani and Horace."

My dad bit his lip. "The firefighters didn't know if you would've made it—" He cleared his throat again. "Out in time."

I made my hands into a small ball. "The chicks?" my dad asked. "Geez, you two. All the chicks made it out. Elliott told me what he did."

I leaned back into the pillows.

My dad gently held my hand. "You two really brought a lot of excitement into my life," he said. "Maybe you can dial that back a little bit."

I smiled and closed my eyes.

"You rest, baby." Then he sniffed a little. "I'm so proud of you."

* * * *

The next time I woke up, I was being transferred to another bed and Lani was with me. "Elliott was released," she said. "But you, my dear, are spending the night." She followed alongside me into the elevator and up to a regular hospital floor. "I convinced your dad that I'd take care of you while he takes Elliott home for dinner and a shower."

I held my own hair out.

"You are getting a shower as soon as possible," she said. "But I'm not sure how much that will help the smell." She waved her hand in front of her face as she followed along with the attendant pushing the bed.

When we waited for an elevator, I grabbed one of her hands with both of mine. "Thank you," I whispered and coughed.

Lani's smile wobbled. "It's the least I can do after getting you into this mess. If I hadn't pushed you…"

I raised my eyebrows and pointed to myself the best I could.

"I know," she said. "You probably would have done it anyway, but I can't help feeling responsible."

I shook my head, which made me feel nauseous. It must have shown on my face because the attendant pushing my hospital bed gave Lani a look.

She pushed down on my shoulder. "Just lay back and rest or you'll get me kicked out." She stayed until I was settled into my room.

"Sharon?" I whispered.

"Oh, she's in jail," she said. "The first fire truck blocked her car in, and Norma saw her as soon as she arrived."

I lifted my hands and gave her a "*what the hell?*" gesture.

"I don't know what she was thinking," Lani said. "But she and Bert are already spilling their guts and trying to pin the murders on each other."

I raised my eyebrows.

"Yeah, can you believe it? That other guy who was murdered was Bert's business partner, Oliver Voss. And get this." She paused for dramatic effect. "He's tall and bald."

My eyebrows shot up.

"I know!" He wasn't bald when they questioned him the night of Twila's murder and he had a thick beard. That's why no one recognized him from your sketch, plus you were kind of off. Anyway, Bert says that Sharon killed Oliver because he blackmailed her. She had to give him all their money or he was going to tell the police she and Bert killed Twila. And Sharon is saying that Bert did it for the same reason."

I heard movement at the door and saw Joss standing there, holding flowers and looking awkward.

"Oh," Lani said. "I have to…" She didn't even finish the sentence, just dashed out of the room.

"I'm so sorry." His voice was thick with guilt. "I had no idea someone could get locked in that chicken coop."

"Not your fault," I whispered, wishing Lani had already arranged my shampoo. I thought about how bloodshot my eyes must be. Maybe Lani could get me a complete makeover. "You couldn't have known a crazy person was after me."

He moved closer. "I can't believe you saved all the chicks."

"You'll have to thank Elliott for that," I said, and coughed. "I was just trying to save him."

He didn't seem to believe me.

"Hey, are you allowed to be here?" I intended it to be a joke, but with my voice barely a whisper it sounded more serious.

He looked down at the floor. "I was going to wait till you were better to talk to you about that." Then he met my eyes. "I decided I have to stop giving into my ex-wife's emotional blackmail. When I heard what almost happened…" He paused, his expression growing intense. "It made me realize I didn't want to lose you. I know that's stupid. We haven't even had a date or anything. But I'm going to fix that, I mean, if you want to."

Then I noticed his pocket move. "What's that?"

"Oh." He brought out a chick, looking over his shoulder to make sure none of the hospital staff saw his contraband. "I thought Elliott would get a kick out of it."

"Aw," I said, as he put the chick in my hand.

It promptly pooped.

* * * *

Elliott and my dad were back right after dinner, and Elliot was delighted to see the chick.

When the nurse left, my dad went out to the waiting room and brought Lani back in with Trouble. I started to cry a little when Lani took her out of the carrier and handed her to me. "My hero," I said. She sniffed me all over and meowed. *You stink but I love you anyway.*

Then she turned her attention to the chick in Elliott's hand.

"I better get this little one home," Joss said.

"Where are you keeping them?" I asked.

"The spare bathroom," he said. "I may never get the smell out of there, but that's where they're staying until I get another coop built."

He patted Elliott on the shoulder. "Thanks again for saving my chicks."

* * * *

Less than a week later, we were all in the Sunnyside Rec Center auditorium waiting for Elliott's play.

The week had been filled with depositions and requests for interviews from across the country. Norma had stopped by often, letting me know about the progress of the case against Bert and Sharon.

Sharon was charged immediately—arson with special circumstances. And every day seemed to bring additional charges as new information was uncovered, including more details about the murders of Twila Jenkins and Oliver Voss. Bert revealed that until a year before, his business had been on the up-and-up. But then Sharon's closet company had taken a hit and he'd lost a big chunk of money in the market, when other companies had not. He'd come up with the scheme of the new fund to cover his losses, and the whole thing had snowballed.

Norma verified that the phone call Twila received the night of the trade show was from Tod Walker. She had asked him to look at the prospectus and treat it as a puzzle. He'd called to let her know that the puzzle didn't work, which is what he told police. As I suspected, Twila confronted Sharon who decided to shut Twila up, permanently, and my Meowio knife was convenient. Then Sharon called her husband to help her clean up the mess.

I really had heard him type in the security code that sounded like Beethoven's Fifth that night. He'd wiped Sharon's fingerprints from the knife and they were driving out when we drove in.

They thought they had the perfect fall guy, or girl.

In the wake of all the publicity, Twomey's Health Food had announced that Meowio Batali's Gourmet Organic Cat Food was going to be sold at their stores. Quincy had sent me a tongue-in-cheek text, *"Congrats on the great marketing idea! All you had to do was almost get burned alive!"* when he heard the news.

I'd texted back, *"Funny! No need for an encore."*

My dad convinced me to allow Quincy to invest and become my official business partner as well as advisor. As soon as everything was back to normal, we were going to start increasing production and go from there. And my dad suggested I ask Elliott if he wanted us to stay in Sunnyside with him for as long as we wanted. "Only if he, and you, want to," he'd said.

Which was smart, because Elliott had said yes, giving us both a way to save face and be together.

Twomey's had taken care of the nasty dude leaving bad reviews. He produced his own organic pet food and thought leaving bad reviews would lead to more business for him. Twomey's lawyers had sent him a cease and desist letter and all the bad posts had disappeared overnight.

Norma had verified what I guessed about Tod, that he was agoraphobic and a total shut-in. He'd loved solving Twila's puzzles.

When I was allowed to drive, I'd gone back to visit him. This time he let me inside the building when I hit the button for 3B. I sat down against the wall by his door.

"You're back," he said through the door. It sounded like he was sitting on the floor too.

"I'm back." I wasn't quite sure what to tell him. "I wanted to thank you for helping me."

"You found Twila," he said. "You figured out who killed her."

"Did you hear that on the news?" I asked.

"Yes," he said. "And Norma told me. I've been calling her. Every day. She answers my questions."

I couldn't help but smile. "She must like you better than me." Even though Norma had finally been telling me what I needed to know.

"She likes you," he said.

"How do you know?"

"She's my friend. She told me you're her friend, too."

* * * *

I was happy to put it all behind me for Elliott's play, something that gave me pure joy. I couldn't stop beaming. Hank sat beside me, with Sue, Annie, Lani, and Piper on one side. Joss and his delightful daughter, Kai, sat on the other side of me. And Kai was chattering away to Norma's daughter with her mom on the end.

The opening, and closing, of the Sunnyside Youth Theater Group's presentation of *Seussical the Musical* finally arrived. All the people who loved Elliott the most were together in the front row. Lani had used her position as costume chair to sneak in and put reserved signs on our seats.

The musical was charming, and the innocence of the children's voices of all ages harmonizing to create beautiful music warmed my heart. The colorful designs of the set and the costumes created the world of Whoville and Jungle of Nool and the other weird and wacky places of Seuss. The actors danced, with varying degrees of grace—the smallest making us all smile at their earnest and cute efforts.

Elliott's voice was lovely, along with all the leads. I was amazed at all the talent these young actors demonstrated, but today, it was more special than ever.

By the end, with the moral of the story shining through, because of Horton's devotion, *A person's a person no matter how small*, there wasn't a dry eye in the house.

I was always emotional during junior theater shows, but after what we'd been through, I was almost overcome. I must have made a sound, because both my dad and Lani reached over to grab my arm and squeeze. They both looked like they were holding back tears too.

I let mine fall but smiled through them. The cast took a bow and then moved to the side to highlight the stars. The entire audience came to their feet in a standing ovation. The look on Elliott's face—pride and joy—would stay with me forever.

My dad grabbed my hand. "Good job," he said, with so much emotion that I knew all the levels he meant, but most important, good job on raising such a great kid.

Elliott scanned the crowd and waved at his little fan club. Then he stared at me, made a little heart with his hands and smiled, his love shining through. I sent a heart back.

I looked up and down the row of Elliott's little fan club and saw the look in Kai's eyes when she watched Elliott and the other actors. Hunger mixed with hero worship. The same look Elliott had at his first musical. Another theater kid was born.

The whole gang headed over to Pico's to celebrate when it was over, even Norma. I looked around. "The only one missing is Trouble," I said.

My dad laughed. "I think we've had enough Trouble for a lifetime."

Don't miss the next book in

The Gourmet Cat Mystery series:

The Trouble with Truth

By

Kathy Krevat

Coming to your favorite booksellers
and e-tailers in

August 2018!

ABOUT THE AUTHOR

Kathy Krevat is the author of the Gourmet Cat Mystery series featuring cat food chef Colbie Summers and her finicky cat Trouble. She also writes the bestselling Chocolate Covered Mystery series under the pen name, Kathy Aarons.

A long-time California resident, Kathy lives in San Diego with her husband of twenty-five years, close to the beach, their two grown daughters, and Philz coffee.

Printed in the United States
by Baker & Taylor Publisher Services